She thought she'd never see him again...

One leap and Beast was out of the bath and down the hall, trailing soapy water, with Layne right behind him. She turned the corner into the living room less than a yard behind the dog and stopped dead when she saw Robbie at the front door. For standing beside her son, one hand on the child's shoulder, was her estranged husband, Kyle Emerson.

Layne's hand went automatically to her hair, and encountered a clump of shampoo suds—one of several places Beast had left his mark. One wet brown strand of hair hung in her eyes. Her low-necked shirt was soaked. Her sandals squeaked with every movement.

Kyle raised a hand to stroke his tie, and his eyes traveled from her head to her toes. "Layne," he said gently, "you haven't changed a bit."

⌁⌁⌁⌁⌁⌁⌁⌁⌁⌁ ⌁ FAMILY ⌁

∧∧∧∧∧∧∧∧∧∧

❧ FAMILY ❧

Leigh MICHAELS

Wednesday's Child

MARRIED
FOR A
MINUTE

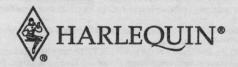

HARLEQUIN®

TORONTO • NEW YORK • LONDON
AMSTERDAM • PARIS • SYDNEY • HAMBURG
STOCKHOLM • ATHENS • TOKYO • MILAN • MADRID
PRAGUE • WARSAW • BUDAPEST • AUCKLAND

HARLEQUIN BOOKS
225 Duncan Mill Road, Don Mills,
Ontario, Canada M3B 3K9

ISBN 0-373-82160-3

WEDNESDAY'S CHILD

Dear Reader,

I'm so pleased to be able to share *Wednesday's Child* with you as part of the FAMILY series. The Emersons—especially Robbie and Beast— have always occupied a special corner of my heart. I think that's partly because they're the family that introduced me to Kansas City, now one of my favorite places, when I went there to research their story.

The other reason this story is so dear to me is that I deeply believe in the power of commitment and communication in marriage. Kyle and Layne's struggle to face their problems and salvage their relationship made them both stronger—just as adversity, faced hand in hand, has strengthened many a marriage in real life.

Families aren't born, they're created. Sometimes that's hard work—but the result is well worth the labor. I wish for you, all my very dear readers, the warmth and love and comfort of *family*.

[signature]

CHAPTER ONE

LAYNE EMERSON opened the oil can and balanced it so it could drain into the motor of her car. She leaned against the fender, brushing a trickle of perspiration away with her finger, unaware of the streak of oil she left on her cheek. The faded green paint on the fender was warm under the brilliant afternoon sun; she could feel the heat through the brief shorts and low-necked top she wore. It was the end of June and the summer was a hot one.

Across the driveway in the neighbouring yard, two small boys wrestled in the grass with a large sheepdog. She watched the trio for a few minutes, then something in their play alarmed her, "Robbie! Tony!" she called. "Don't tease the dog like that!"

One of the boys looked up. "Oh, Mom," Robbie said, "Beast wouldn't bite me." But he got up from the grass, dusted his shorts off, and found a stick which he tossed for the dog to retrieve.

He was probably right, Layne thought. Beast was the gentlest of all creatures, and he had never turned on his owner, but he was so enormous next to her small son that she had to fear for Robbie sometimes. Being a single parent was really difficult, she thought. She didn't know sometimes if there was anything she was doing right. Being wholly responsible for an eight-year-old was a constant drain.

It was, however, she thought, better than being without the eight-year-old. Robbie was not only her son, but her sunshine.

Beast brought the stick and dropped it at her feet, his tongue hanging out and his beady eyes sparkling in anticipation. For once, the thick hair that usually hid his eyes had blown back, and his vision was unhindered.

"I'm not the one who throws sticks, dummy," she told him. "I'm just the one who buys the dog food." Beast reared up and put his paws on her shoulders, and Layne got a whiff of the dog's coat. "Robbie!" she called. "This dog needs a bath!"

Robbie came across the driveway and tossed the stick again. Beast romped off after it, and Robbie said, "Sure, Mom. I'll give him a bath tomorrow." Then he gave her a cheeky grin. "You need one too, Mom. You've got oil on your face. Are you almost finished working on The Tank?"

Layne raised a hand to wipe the oil off, and only succeeded in smearing it further. "Almost. At least I'll have finished everything I can do."

"Do you have to work today?" he asked.

"Mr Hamburg brought me some more of his life story to type. But it can wait till this evening if you have plans." She smiled at him and ruffled his dark hair. "What do you want to do? Bake cookies?"

"Not today. Will you come to my Little League game this afternoon? You missed last week."

"Yes, I'll come. But you know I had to go to that job interview last week. It was very important."

"It couldn't have been too important," Robbie argued. "You didn't get the job."

"Even if I didn't, I had to try."

Robbie scuffled his shoes in the dirt. "I don't want

you to go back to work in some old office. And I don't want to go to day care.''

"I know you don't, Robbie. But someone has to hold a job around here to pay the rent and the grocery bill. And eight years old just isn't big enough to stay alone.''

"Yeah, sure.'' But Robbie's voice was plainly unhappy.

Layne didn't try to explain any further. She had tried so many times, and it always seemed to end up the same. Robbie loathed day care. It was the main reason she had so hated to lose her last job; as the secretary to a school head she had worked much the same hours as Robbie was in school, and she had even had the same holidays. But the funding for her position had run out, and there would be no job next autumn. She wasn't looking forward to going back to a nine-to-five office, either—but someone had to put the food on the table. Even the school job hadn't left much for extras; they certainly couldn't live indefinitely without a paycheque of some kind.

So she hugged Robbie and ruffled his black hair, and turned to check the oil can to see if it was empty. The Tank seemed to drink oil. But it was transportation, she reminded herself, even if it was old and used too much petrol and was rusting out.

"Dad's picture was in this morning's paper,'' Robbie said.

Layne kept her face turned away and her voice carefully casual. "Was it?'' She checked the tension on the fan belt.

"Yeah. They opened North Winds Shopping Mall yesterday. He was the one who built it, you know. Emco had all the contracts.'' There was pride in his voice.

"Yes, I know.'' She thought, How could I avoid

knowing? Robbie had watched the progress of that construction for the past two years. He hadn't missed a single news item about it. North Winds was the prototype of a new approach to shopping mall construction; it was supposed to sweep the country within ten years. So it wasn't surprising that when dedication day came around, the man who had built it would be asked to cut the official ribbon. She should have expected it.

The man who had built everything worth knowing about in the Kansas City area for the last five years. Kyle Emerson, the head of Emco, which, as Robbie had told her so often, was the biggest construction company in the Midwest.

Why, Layne asked herself, had she ever told Robbie about his father? And then she reminded herself that she hadn't actually told him at all. Robbie had made the connection himself two years ago. The fact that a first-grader had been so quick to draw a perfectly accurate conclusion had startled her so that she had confirmed his suspicions before she had even paused to think. If she had only taken that extra moment...

Robbie had been home from school, suffering from a virus. He had been watching the noon news while waiting for the cartoons to start, when Kyle Emerson had been interviewed about his new shopping centre project. Robbie had been transfixed then he had called, "Mom! Come see this guy who looks just like me!"

And as Layne, without any warning, found herself face to face with the image of Kyle Emerson, Robbie had said, "His name is Emerson, too. Is he my father?"

And Layne had murmured, "Yes, Robbie."

She could kick herself now, of course. If she could have foreseen what Robbie would do, she might have lied to him. For instantly he had become a TV news freak and the youngest steady reader of the *Kansas City Star*, searching for the next mention of Kyle Emerson for his scrapbook.

Robbie's playmate had gone back into his house next door, and now his mother leaned out of the casement window above her kitchen sink and called, "Hey, you two, I just took chocolate chip cookies out of the oven."

"Can I go have some?" Robbie asked, "Clare makes the best cookies."

"Better than ours?" she teased.

"Heck, no. But next best. And she makes them more often."

Layne laughed. "Sure, Rob. Tell Clare I'll be there in a minute." She checked the water in the battery, and fingered the cable connections, and wished that she had told Robbie that there were hundreds of men named Emerson in Kansas City, and that she'd never heard of one named Kyle.

The casement window opened again. "You'd better hurry, Layne," Clare Reynolds called. "Your coffee is poured."

Layne slammed the hood of The Tank and crossed the driveway. Clare was already sitting at the kitchen table with her coffee. She pushed Layne's cup and the plate of cookies towards her.

"The boys took their snack to the rec room," she said. "Which leaves you free to tell me what that gloomy expression on your face means. What's wrong, Layne?"

"Nothing. Everything." Layne bit into a cookie, and still-melting chocolate chips oozed out. "There are no job prospects yet, and it's really beginning to bother me. I thought I had it all planned, and we've been careful what we spent ever since I found out I'd be laid off. But it just takes more money than I figured on."

"It has a habit of doing that," Clare said. "Is there any possibility the school district will call you back?"

"Perhaps. But I'm afraid to count on it, Clare. What if they don't have an opening? They won't, unless someone retires or takes another job. And there just aren't many secretarial positions in the schools."

Clare nodded. "I know. What about the private typing business?"

"It's picking up. I even made a hundred dollars last week on a book manuscript."

"Only a hundred?"

"It was a short book. That paid for the repairs The Tank had to have last month. And there is always Mr Hamburg's life story; it must be going into the third volume."

"Now if he'll just pay you," Clare said dryly. "I put up some more flyers yesterday when I was shopping."

"I keep thinking that perhaps we can make it through the summer on what the typing will bring in. After all, the bills aren't as big."

"Come to think of it, I have a friend who belongs to a writers' club. I'll call her. It might not be a book a week, but there should be something." Clare stirred her coffee moodily. "Robbie seems happy to have you at home."

"Of course he is. He hates it when I go for interviews or even talk about getting another job. It's one long continual battle."

"Having you home so much has spoiled him."

"That's not all—it spoiled me too. Being off work at three every afternoon was awful nice. I don't want to go back to a regular job any more than Robbie wants me to."

"Layne, is something bothering him?"

"Nothing more than the idea of going back to day care, as far as I know." She sipped her coffee and added reluctantly, "He's talking about his father again."

Clare got up and refilled her cup. "He's a boy, Layne. And he's old enough to realise that even the kids who have divorced parents see their dads once in a while."

"So does Robbie," Layne muttered sarcastically. "In the newspaper, which he reads word-for-word every day."

"Robbie doesn't understand why he never sees his dad. So he talks about him to prove that Kyle isn't just in his imagination."

"You make it sound so simple, Clare."

"Did you see the picture?" Clare reached for the newspaper on the counter.

"No. I can live without the experience." But Layne took it. The story was at the top of the front page, with a banner headline; North Winds was an important development, and it had received nationwide publicity. She didn't want to look at the photograph, but another part of her couldn't look away. There in living colour on the front page was Kyle, his black hair ruffling in the breeze as he cut the ribbon across the main doors of the North Winds Mall.

He hadn't changed, Layne told herself. Oh, that might be a trace of white in the hair at his temples—it was difficult to tell in the grainy newspaper photo. And there were two deep lines between his eyes as he frowned over the wide red ribbon. But otherwise, everything was the same. He was still as devastatingly handsome as he had been nine years ago.

And there was another thing that hadn't changed, Layne told herself as she looked closer at the photograph. Beside him was Jessica Tate, one hand raised to keep her wide-brimmed hat from fluttering off in the breeze, the other under Kyle's on the big shears. She was smiling, and she was beautiful.

The agony of that last afternoon at Wheatlands swept over Layne in waves. That afternoon that Jessica Tate had told her the truth...

Layne pushed the hurt to the back of her mind and read the caption. Jessica owned a string of boutiques, including a new one in North Winds Mall. To most people, it would explain why she was beside Kyle, acting as if she belonged there. Layne knew better.

Clare propped her hands on the table and rested her chin on them. "Why don't you call Kyle?" she asked gently. "I can't believe that he would want you and Robbie to be living like this. And he can certainly afford to pay child support."

"Not if he's entertaining Jessica Tate, he can't," Layne snapped. "That lady is expensive. And you know that if he finds out about Robbie, he'll take him away from me."

Clare took a deep breath. "Would that be so awful for Robbie?" she asked gently.

"Robbie is a gifted child, Clare! He's a brilliant child!"

"I know that. That's exactly what I mean. He needs additional advantages that you can't give him. You can't send him to private school, Layne, or to summer camp. And what about college? I know it's a long way off, but surely you want the best for Robbie. What can you give him, compared to what his father can do for him?"

"I can love him!" Layne cried. "Love him because he's Robbie, not just because he's an Emerson!" She buried her head in her arms on the table. Great choking sobs tore at her throat.

Clare sighed and lit a cigarette. She tapped it on the edge of the crystal ashtray and waited for Layne's sobs to quiet. Then she patted her friend's shoulder. "I'm sorry, honey. You're right, of course. But I hurt so, watching you struggle to provide for Robbie when Kyle could do it so easily. When he ought to be doing it." She stroked Layne's glossy brown hair.

"What's the matter, Mom?" Robbie asked at Layne's elbow.

She raised her head and gave him a watery smile. "Oh, honey, sometimes I just get scared when I think about things."

"Oh." He thought that over for a moment and dismissed it. "Are you still coming to the game?"

"Is it time?" Layne glanced at her watch. "Run home and get your uniform on. We'll have to hurry."

Robbie ducked out the door. Layne dashed a hand across her eyes, where tears still pooled. "Clare…"

"I know. I'm sorry, and I won't bring it up again, even though I think…" She stopped and shook her head. "I'll try not to bring it up," she said ruefully. "All right? Now you'd better hurry, too. And wash the streak of oil off your cheek before you go!"

Layne sat down on the top bleacher, off in a corner by herself. She didn't feel like being near anyone; the tears had been too recent, and she was afraid that they might start again if anybody so much as asked her what was new.

Down on the field, Robbie's team, the Angels, was warming up. Their blue-and-gold uniforms stood out against the red and white of the opposing team. She saw Robbie talking to his coach, then the man looked up at the stands and waved at Layne. She waved back, pushed her dark glasses up, and hoped that he wouldn't come up to say hello just now. She hated to have anyone see her cry, and if Gary Spencer showed an ounce of concern or sympathy she'd break down all over again.

So she watched the team warm up. Robbie seemed so young to be in organised sports, Layne thought, but he adored baseball, so she had given in. At least he hadn't chosen a violent sport like football.

She had not been surprised that baseball had been Robbie's choice, for hadn't Kyle told her once that it was the sport of gentlemen? Emco's employees had a team, that summer so long ago. Kyle played shortstop, and he'd taken her to all the games. Layne, at seventeen, had been so blinded by his charm that she wouldn't have cared if he had expected her to be third base, as long as she could be with him.

Yes, she thought, Robbie was definitely his father's son. No wonder he had been so certain the day he'd first seen Kyle on the television screen.

The team's coach was beside her before she was aware he was near. "I'm glad you're here, Layne," Gary said. "Rob really missed you last week. He stole second base, you know, and he wanted you to see him."

"He told me. He was very proud of himself."

"The boy has the makings of a good athlete. If he keeps developing as he has over the past year, I wouldn't be surprised to see him a star on my high-school team. And then who knows?"

"I think eight years old is a little young to be signing him with the Royals, Gary," Layne said tartly.

Her response startled him. "Well, yes. But I can dream, can't I? I don't say anything to him about it."

"I didn't mean to be sharp with you. But I've never

been very comfortable about baseball being a profession."

"I see what you mean. Half my team thinks they're going to be stars in pro ball," Gary mused. "Is something wrong, Layne? You look a little unusual."

Layne self-consciously straightened her dark glasses and looked out over the field. "It's just been a hard day."

Gary looked relieved. "I'm glad it isn't anything I did. I'll take you and Robbie out for a pizza after the game."

"Shouldn't we see what the score is, first?"

"Why? If Robbie isn't celebrating a victory, he'll need consolation for a loss."

Layne smiled reluctantly. Gary was good for her, she admitted; sometimes he almost forced her into doing things, but she always ended up enjoying herself. "You're right. And Robbie can always eat pizza."

Gary glanced down at the field. "I'd better get down to my boys. I'm shirking my duties."

The game started, and Layne watched the action with only half her mind. She was remembering other days, and other games.

It seemed to her that fully half of Kyle's brief courtship had taken place at the ballpark. Either he was on the field and Layne was watching from the bleachers, or they were in the stands at the professional games, eating hot dogs and cheering Kyle's favourites. Layne hadn't cared who won or lost, but she minded very much when he was unhappy.

Baseball had never been her passion. She was certain, however, that Kyle had never suspected her lack of interest in the sport. She had bought books, learned to read base scores, studied all the players, in an effort to be what he wanted her to be.

It wouldn't have mattered what he wanted to do. If Kyle had wanted to hunt elephants in darkest Africa, she thought, she would have been waiting at his elbow to hold his gun. Layne had been so thrilled at seventeen to be noticed by the older, handsome and frankly sexy Kyle that she would have done anything to please him.

How very much she had grown up over the last eight years, she thought a little sadly. She couldn't help wondering just a bit what Kyle would think of her now. Had he missed the little wife who would have breathed for him if it had only been possible? After all, the honeymoon had scarcely been over. Or had he been relieved when she disappeared from his life?

Had her clinging love smothered him? That's funny, Layne thought. The idea had never occurred to her before.

Robbie hit safely into right field and easily beat the throw to first base, hitching up his uniform with a flair as the ball arrived ten seconds after him.

"He's a bit of a showoff," Layne muttered as he looked towards the dugout for approval. Gary must have supplied it, for Robbie pulled his cap down tight over his ears with a swagger, turned his attention to the pitcher, and paced off a two-yard lead towards second base. Layne watched him, but her thoughts were in the past.

She had adored Kyle so blindly that it never occurred to her to wonder just what it was about her that he found attractive. He'd actually treated her like a little sister much of the time, dragging her along on his outings with the guys. He had said that being alone with her was too much temptation. Had he been telling the truth?

Why, she wondered now, had she not questioned his reasons when he asked her to marry him? But she had been so eager to be his wife that nothing could have stopped her.

A world of illusion it was that she had lived in, she knew now. Jessica Tate had left her illusions in shreds that dreadful day in the library at Wheatlands.

A cheer went up from the crowd, and Layne's attention snapped back to the field. Robbie had stolen second base; he was dusting the dirt collected by his slide off his uniform. He retrieved his cap and took a graceful bow towards the stands.

"What a little actor!" Layne told herself. And no wonder that his uniform was so hard to keep clean. It was one gigantic streak of dirt up the left side. Thank heaven whoever was in charge of uniforms hadn't chosen white ones.

The inning ended with Robbie stranded at third, and the Angels took the field. The game dragged on, and Layne yawned in the stands. The sun beat down mercilessly, and she wished that she had remembered to pick up her suntan lotion. She brushed a hand experimentally across the back of her neck; the skin felt hot and tight.

Kyle used to tease her about how easily she sunburned. It was amazing, he used to say, that he was actually the fair-skinned one, but he tanned and she burned. But that was because of all the hours he'd spent in the sun in the days when he was just a construction worker instead of the owner of the business...

Why was she wasting so much time thinking about Kyle today? Layne asked herself, and decided that it was only because Robbie had brought the subject up.

It was Robbie's turn at bat again, and this time he scarcely beat the throw to first base. But the umpire signalled that he was safe, and Robbie pulled his cap down tight and took his lead off the base.

"The little brat is going to try it again," Layne thought, and watched half-admiringly as Robbie inched himself into a position to steal. The pitcher eyed him suspiciously before going into his wind-up. The instant the ball was released, Robbie was off in a blur of blue-and-gold uniform and dust from the path, sliding the last six feet into second base—and the second baseman. The crowd went wild. Even the opposing team's fans realised that here was something unusual and cheered the accomplishment.

It was close, so close that the umpire hadn't yet ruled when Robbie popped back to his feet. Then, it seemed to Layne, two things happened simultaneously. The umpire swept his arms out to signal that Robbie had made it in time, and the child dropped to the ground in a heap like a rag doll tossed aside by a child at play.

Layne broke the Little League record for fastest time in the downhill bleachers and reached the field only an instant behind Gary. She peered over the coach's shoulder at her son's face. He'd lost his cap somewhere on the run, and his dark hair was rumpled. The freckles that dusted his nose stood out like puddles against paper-white skin, and his eyes were dark with pain.

"Mom?" he questioned with a catch in his voice.

"I'm right here, Robbie." Layne took his hand, and Robbie sighed and closed his eyes against the pain.

"It's his ankle, Layne," Gary said. His eyes met hers; they were full of concern.

"A sprain?"

"Probably. But I think we should have it X-rayed. Where's your car?"

"It's right by the gate."

"I'll bring Robbie." He cradled the child in his arms and carried him to The Tank, carefully strapping him into the front seat. "I'd come with you, but…"

"That's all right. The rest of the boys need you."

"I'll stop by the house after the game to see how he is."

"Thanks, Gary," Layne was shaking a little as she started the car. This was exactly what she didn't need right now, she thought. Emergency room, X-rays—and no insurance to cover the cost. Why had Robbie tried that darn fool stunt? she thought, and then scolded herself, Robbie hadn't done it on purpose.

He looked a little better; the colour was starting to come back to his face. "How are you feeling, Rob?" she asked.

"It hurts, Mom. When I tried to get up, my foot just wouldn't hold me." He winced. "Was I safe?"

"You were safe."

Robbie cheered up. "That's okay then. Gary can put in a pinch runner. He'll probably pick Tom because he's the fastest runner on the team. After me, that is."

"I'm sure Gary will figure something out."

An orderly saw them coming and met them with a wheelchair. Robbie was already in the radiology department by the time Layne had the forms filled out, and she sat in the waiting room, her hands clenched, till the X-rays were completed.

Robbie chattered as the orderly wheeled him back down the hall. "I broke my record," he bragged. "The most I ever stole before was one base in a game. Today I got two." His leg was propped up on the chair's footrest. "Isn't this neat, Mom? They took pictures of my ankle."

Layne didn't trust herself to answer.

A few minutes later a young man in a lab coat came down the hall. "Mrs Emerson?" he said, and Layne thought he looked slightly surprised when she answered. Let him wonder, she thought. She was young to be the mother of an eight-year-old, and the shorts and low-necked top she wore didn't make her look any older. She followed him into an office where an X-ray hung on a light box.

"All Robbie cares about is that he broke his record," she said, a little nervously.

He glanced at her and flipped a switch. "Yes. Well, he also broke his ankle." He took a pen from his pocket and pointed out a faint shadow on the X-ray. "Right here. He did a good job of it, too. He'll need to be in a cast four to six weeks."

Layne sat down abruptly in the nearest chair. "That will kill him. Isn't there any alternative?"

"None, I imagine he'll adjust quickly. Most kids do. By the second day there isn't anyplace they won't go on their crutches. If it's any consolation, it would be more painful if he'd just sprained it, and ligaments are slower to heal than bone is. As it is, a month or so and he'll be good as new." He turned the light box off. "Do you want to tell him, or shall I?"

"You may have the pleasure." No baseball, no swimming, no running about the neighbourhood... It was going to be a very long month.

"I'll refer you to an orthopaedic surgeon..."

"Surgeon?" Layne's voice was sharp with alarm.

"That doesn't mean Robbie needs surgery, Mrs Emerson, but you should have the fracture X-rayed again in a week or so to be sure it's healing properly. The doctor can do that right in his office, through the cast. Then he'll give you a better idea of when the cast can be removed. We specialise in putting plaster on around here, not taking it off.'' He gave Layne a crooked smile and a slip of paper.

She looked at it. ''Are his fees expensive?''

The young doctor looked surprised. ''Yes, I suppose they are,'' he said. ''Most specialists are. You could take him to your own family doctor, of course, and perhaps it would be a little cheaper. But if it were my kid, I'd go for the best. He's only eight years old. You want somebody taking care of that fracture who can make sure he won't have lasting damage.''

Layne nodded and tucked the slip of paper in the pocket of her shorts. Oh, Robbie, she thought, what in heaven are we going to do?

CHAPTER TWO

THE specialist's examining room was large and plush, and to Layne the design in the wallpaper looked like dollar signs. Robbie hopped up on to the end of the table and handed his crutches to his mother. "This is neat, Mom," he said. "And it's kind of fun to get my ankle X-rayed. How do they do it through the cast?" He studied the plaster, decorated with a week's worth of autographs and artwork, as though he expected to find the answer engraved there.

"I don't know, Robbie." Her voice was sharp, and then Layne caught herself. He was being such a good sport about the whole thing; what was the matter with her? He had shed a few tears as the cast went on, and a few more when he had to watch his first game ever from the dugout, but on the whole he had taken to the cast easily. The young resident at the hospital had been correct; two days and Robbie had been all over the neighbourhood on his crutches. Steps were no challenge at all, though Layne still watched with her heart in her mouth as he dashed up and down. The one who had really suffered from it all was Beast, who didn't understand why his playmate couldn't wrestle or run any more.

"Mrs Emerson?" The young nurse looked around the door and smiled at Robbie, who grinned back. "Doctor would like to see you in his office, please." She patted Robbie's shoulder. "How are you doing, Tiger?"

Layne swallowed hard, and picked up her handbag. "Stay right here, Robbie," she ordered.

"So where would I go?" he complained. "You put my crutches clear over in the corner."

Dr Morgan was tall, thin, and intense, and looked as if he wasted no time on pleasantries. But he surprised Layne by holding a chair for her, then he retreated behind his desk, folded his hands, and rested his chin thoughtfully on his fingertips as he studied her.

She shifted a little uneasily under his scrutiny.

"I'm sure you saw Robbie's X-rays at the hospital," Dr Morgan began.

"Yes—but I didn't pay much attention, I'm afraid. I have no experience with X-rays."

"I have them here." He got up again and posted a sheet of film on a light box on the wall. "The fracture is right here. I don't know if they pointed out this small bone chip?"

"No. I don't think the resident said…"

The doctor put another X-ray beside the first. "Here is the film we took just a few minutes ago," he said, and pointed out the area of the fracture. Then he sat down on the corner of his desk. "The bone chip has turned, Mrs Emerson, and it is not healing."

Layne bit her lip.

"It's lucky that the hospital recommended you to bring him here. If you hadn't, we would have taken the cast off in four weeks, and then started all over. As it is, we can schedule him for surgery right away…"

"Surgery!" Her big eyes widened even more.

"Yes. We'll have to go into the fracture, pin that bone chip back into place, and then put on another cast." He watched the expressions play over her face, and added, with a more kindly note, "It isn't anything Robbie did,

Mrs Emerson. The chip turned at the time the fracture occurred, and there was no way to get it back into place. It isn't the hospital's fault, either; it's only by comparing the two X-rays that I can see it. Even if it had shown up right away, it would have required surgery to repair it.''

"Oh,God.'' Layne put her face in her hands. Glossy brown hair spilled forward over her face. "I don't have insurance…''

"Perhaps you should talk to the people down at the welfare office,'' he suggested. "I'll call the hospital and get a time set up for surgery…''

Welfare? she thought. Never! "Can't we wait a few days? See if it might heal by itself?'' Layne pleaded.

"Mrs Emerson, I don't think you understand. If Robbie is to walk normally, he must have that bone chip pinned. It can't heal itself because it isn't in the right position. You don't have a choice.'' His voice wasn't unkind, but it was firm, and he picked up the telephone as he spoke.

Layne rubbed her temples, trying to massage away the headache that had suddenly struck. It felt as if a mountain had toppled on to her shoulders.

Maybe Clare is right, she thought suddenly. Kyle might help…

But he would take Robbie away from her, without an instant's hesitation. Little Robbie, who had been her one reason for living in those dark days after she had learned the truth about her marriage.

Welfare might not be so bad after all, she thought.

Dr Morgan put the telephone down. "He'll need to be in the hospital Wednesday evening for surgery Thursday morning. I know waiting for a couple of days won't be easy on anyone, but that's the best I can do for a non-emergency case. There's a shortage of operating rooms in this city right now.'' He studied her face. ''I'll tell Robbie. Would you rather wait here?''

Robbie was small and quiet in his corner of the front seat on the way home. Neither of them said a word until Layne parked The Tank in the driveway. Then Robbie, hesitatingly, said, ''Mom, I can get a paper route to help out...''

''And just how do you plan to carry newspapers and use crutches at the same time? Or were you planning to pedal your bike with one foot?'' The questions were sharper than she intended, and Robbie shrank back into his corner, his eyes pooling with tears.

Layne bit her tongue. The child was already frightened; why had she added her anger to his load? She walked around the car and got his crutches out of the back seat.

Robbie struggled out of the car. ''I didn't do it on purpose, Mom,'' he said with quiet dignity.

She put her arms around him and he burrowed his head against her, his eyes squeezed shut to block the tears. ''I know it isn't your fault, Robbie,'' she murmured, her voice choked. ''I love you, baby. It'll be all right. We'll make it somehow.''

Robbie hopped away, and Layne watched him cross the driveway to the back door. He was probably going to his room to cry it out, she thought. And who wouldn't want to? She had found him more than once in the last week lying across his bed, his arms wrapped around Beast's neck, tears creeping out from under tightly closed eyelids. She hadn't had the heart to remind either of them that Beast was not allowed on the bed.

Clare was lying in a lounge chair on her patio with a

box of chocolates and a glass of iced tea. She turned a page of her magazine and waved a lazy hand at Layne. "You look somewhat like the camel who just saw the last straw coming," she said, and pointed at a chair. "Sit down and tell me about it."

Layne collapsed into the chair, envying Clare her suntan lotion and brief swimsuit. Her own linen skirt and sleeveless top felt hot and sticky.

"Have a caramel," Clare recommended. "You'll regret it next time you step on the scale, but it's worth it today." She looked up as a car pulled into Layne's driveway and stopped behind The Tank. "She's over here, Gary!" she called.

Gary pulled up another chair and dropped into it with a sigh. "This has to be the hottest day of the summer," he complained. "But the boys didn't seem to feel a thing. I must be getting old." He unsnapped his Angels shirt and let the breeze cool his chest.

"I wish I could do that," Layne complained.

"Go ahead. I promise not to watch," Gary told her.

"So what did the doctor say?" Clare asked, and pushed the box of chocolates towards Gary.

"Robbie's ankle isn't healing," Layne said flatly. "He will have surgery on Thursday."

There was thirty seconds of absolute silence on the patio. Then Clare said, "Damn."

"It's just my luck, isn't it?" Layne said bitterly. "Eight years old and he's never needed so much as a cut stitched until the day I don't have medical insurance."

"So this whole week has gone for nothing?" Gary asked.

"Unless you count wearing a cast as an educational experience. We start over on Thursday morning."

"What are you going to do, Layne?"

"I suppose I'll plead with the hospital to be decent for once and let me pay it off when I get a job. The doctor suggested I call the welfare office." She didn't look at Clare; she knew what would be reflected in the woman's eyes. And she would not call Kyle. Better to have to work the rest of her life to pay off this debt than to take the chance of losing Robbie.

Gary said, "I'll ask the team's sponsors if they'll help, Layne. They're responsible, after all."

"But they aren't, Gary."

"I bet they'll help anyway. And we'll have a fundraiser to help pay Robbie's bills. The boys will probably like it. It could have happened to any of them."

"Thanks, Gary." Layne glanced at her watch and stood up. "I'd better get supper started. I doubt Robbie is any hungrier than I am, but I suppose we have to eat."

"Let me take you out, Layne."

"I wouldn't be very good company."

"I don't care about that. You deserve a break. Sorry— bad choice of words."

Layne smiled reluctantly. "I don't know about Robbie, though. He may not be at his most pleasant. He was moody all the way home."

"Of course. The poor child is scared." Gary searched through Clare's box of caramels till he found a chocolate one. He offered the box to Layne.

She shook her head. "It's no wonder that he's scared, I suppose. He's never even been admitted to a hospital before."

"Why don't you leave him with me tonight, honey," Clare suggested. "We're having lasagna. It's no trouble to put an extra plate on the table. And I think you need to get out, and away from Robbie."

"It might be a good idea for him to get away from me, too," Layne mused. "All right, Gary. Let me change my clothes."

"You don't need to. I'm not very elegant," Gary said and waved a hand at his Angels uniform and running shoes. "I'm not going to take you to any fancy place."

"I thought for certain that you had reservations at Felicity's," Layne teased. "I want to change, Gary; I'm hot and sticky, I'll be back in a minute."

Robbie was lying on his stomach in front of the television set, the cast propped up on a pillow. He shot a look up at Layne as she came through the room, then turned his attention back to the cartoon.

He looks guilty, Layne thought, and a sudden rush of love came over her. He's only eight, she thought. This is an awful burden for him, and he's afraid to talk to me. He's afraid to tell me even how scared he must be of having surgery, because all I've been talking about is the money.

She sank down on her knees beside him and held out her arms. Robbie uttered a half-sob, half-groan, and flung himself against her, nearly knocking her over. They sat there together on the floor for a long time.

Finally, she hugged him again and said, "You're invited to have lasagna over at Clare's tonight."

"What are you doing?"

"Gary's taking me out."

"He takes you out a lot lately," Robbie mused as he followed her down the hall to her bedroom.

Layne was startled by the note of unhappiness in his voice. "I thought you liked Gary."

"I do—for a coach. But he thinks he's going to be my dad. He isn't, is he?"

"Not that I'm aware of," Layne said warily. "Has he told you that?"

"Oh, not right out. But I can tell. He acts like he's trying to convince me that he'd be an okay stepfather."

Layne started to brush her hair. "And you're not convinced?"

"Heck no. Nobody's ever going to take the place of my real dad." Robbie's voice was definite.

Layne winced. What place was that, she wondered. Just what place in a small boy's life did he reserve for the father he had never met?

"You're always going out with Gary," Robbie pointed out. "And you don't go out with anybody else."

"I like him. He's fun to be with, Robbie. But that doesn't mean I'm going to marry him."

"Well, you'd better not," Robbie announced fiercely.

"Do you feel abandoned when I go out with Gary?" Layne asked lightly.

"No. But Clare doesn't have to baby-sit, you know. I can take care of myself."

Layne dropped a kiss on the top of his head. "I know. So why don't we just agree that the babysitting is for my benefit, and not for yours?"

Robbie thought it over. Then he grinned and flung his arms around her. "All right, Mom. That means I've got the only mother on the block who needs a babysitter!"

Sunshine poured in through the big kitchen window and played around Layne's head. An observer with a bent for poetry might have said that it looked like a halo above the glossy brown hair; Layne would have laughed. But there was no such observer. Robbie sat across the table from her, but he was too deeply absorbed in his corn flakes to pay any attention to poetic imagery this morning. Even Beast was more interested in his breakfast than in Layne.

She held her coffee mug in both hands, elbows propped on the table, and watched her son. Robbie seemed to be back to normal, last night's fears forgotten. Layne knew it couldn't be quite that easy, but she nevertheless envied his attitude. He was certain that somehow, things would work out. She wished she could be as calm.

She studied him, his head bent so far over the cereal bowl that the black eyelashes seemed to lie on his cheeks. One well-shaped hand busily spooned corn flakes, the other turned pages of a book now and then. It was computers again this morning, she concluded, Robbie was trying to teach himself to program a computer to play games. He'd really like to have a computer, but he had stopped reminding her of how much he wanted one about the time she had lost her job.

He was so fearfully handsome, this son of hers, Layne thought, and longed to reach out to stroke his hair, warm in the sunlight that brought out blue highlights in the black. The stunning good looks of the Black Irish, she thought, rarely found these days in such pure form. Kyle's good looks, she reminded herself. It was as if she herself had nothing to do with the formation of this child; he might as well have been a carbon copy of his father. No wonder Robbie had been so certain, when he saw Kyle on the television screen that day, who he was.

Robbie looked up suddenly and she was startled, as she always was, by the improbably deep blue of his eyes. Never had she expected her child to be blue-eyed. Didn't a brown-eyed parent always have brown-eyed children? But she must have a blue-eyed gene somewhere, and so Robbie had inherited Kyle's eyes, too. Some days it almost made her angry, that nowhere in Robbie could she see a single physical feature of hers.

But he has inherited your gentleness, she told herself firmly. That could not have come from Kyle, who didn't know what compassion meant, Kyle could never have cried over a baby robin who fell from the nest. Robbie had, yesterday, and then had carefully buried the broken little body.

"Why are you staring at me?" Robbie asked.

"Was I? I'm sorry." Layne reached for the coffeepot and refilled her mug. It would be the last pound of coffee she could afford to buy, she reminded herself as she sniffed the aromatic brew. Coffee was not a necessity, and so she would do without it. Each dollar she could save would make it easier to get through the summer.

"You always tell me it isn't polite to stare," Robbie pointed out.

"I know. It must have been that you look exceptionally handsome this morning."

Robbie considered that, and then went straight to the heart of the matter. "You're still worried, aren't you?"

Layne stirred her coffee. "Of course I am."

"Wouldn't Dad help us? With the money, I mean?"

"He might. But I'm not going to ask him, and that's the last time I want to hear the subject mentioned. All right, Rob?"

"All right," Robbie said reluctantly, and instantly Layne felt a pang of guilt. Robbie didn't understand why she never wanted to talk about Kyle. It hadn't been necessary to be quite so abrupt with him.

Beast licked the bottom of his dish, took a long slurp from his water bowl, and returned hopefully to the food dish, half-expecting that someone might have refilled it while his back was turned. When his nose encountered only emptiness, he lumbered across the kitchen and nudged Layne's hand, spilling her coffee. She set the cup down with an exclamation.

"Darn it, Beast! Robbie, can't you do something with this dog? All he does is eat and aggravate me these days."

"I can't walk him, Mom. I tried, but he pulls me off my feet."

"Well, see if Tony will. He's eating like a horse and getting as big as one too, with no exercise."

Beast took her words as encouragement. He reared up to grin in her face, and Layne recoiled. "And he never got his promised bath either," she reminded.

"I'd do it, Mom, but he'll get my cast all wet."

"Then you may do the breakfast dishes instead, Robbie, and I'll bathe the dog. Because we aren't both staying in this house in this condition," she told Beast, who grinned again and tried to wash her face with his tongue.

"I'd do dishes if we can bake a cake later," Robbie bargained. "Chocolate, maybe?"

"Maybe. But I have to get to work on Mr Hamburg's life story. I've been putting it off, and he's going to be bringing another instalment any day now."

"He's a pain. Why do you work for him?"

"Because no matter how much he complains, he eventually pays my price. And quit postponing the dishes. I'm not going to forget about them."

Robbie started to run dishwater, then turned the taps off. "Here comes Gary," he announced. "Can I wait till after he goes home? How was your date last night?"

Layne groaned. "You entertain Gary," she suggested. "And tell him that I have already started Beasts's bath, and cannot be interrupted."

"The date wasn't so good, huh?" Robbie concluded.

Layne didn't answer. She grabbed the dog by the collar and dragged him into the bathroom.

"Darn Gary anyhow," she muttered as she started the hot water running in the bath. And darn Robbie. If he hadn't told her that Gary was acting like a stepfather, she probably would never have noticed. But Robbie had said it, and Layne had found herself looking for hidden meaning in everything Gary had talked about last night.

And she had found it. Gary's tone when he talked about Robbie was just a little too conciliating, a little too favourable, to be that of a mere friend.

She had always enjoyed Gary's company, since the day he first showed up at her desk at the high school. He taught social studies and coached wrestling and baseball, and since the day he first saw Layne he had always seemed to have an errand in the office. When he discovered she had a son, he hadn't rested until he had diagnosed Robbie's potential as a Little Leaguer. He had been exactly what Layne needed—a friend who was always there to listen, a man who helped her understand that all men were not like Kyle, and a male who made himself an uncle to Robbie.

But she had never considered him as a possible husband. Gary was a survivor of a bad marriage, too, and Layne had assumed that he was as unwilling as she to try again. But he had made it clear last night that he expected it to be only a matter of time before they were married. It was all in the nicest possible way, of course. No pressure, just confidence that she agreed with him.

And now Layne was faced with a dilemma. It was natural that he thought that; she had not dated anyone else in the year that she had known him. But marriage to Gary—or, indeed, marriage to anyone—had never crossed her mind, and she wasn't sure she wanted to think about it now. She had tried to tell him that last night, but Gary had just smiled.

The water steamed gently in the bath, and she looked from it to Beast, who was huddled in the corner of the bathroom trying to make himself invisible. His head was hunched and his eyes were hidden behind the long hair. He apparently thought that if he couldn't see Layne, she couldn't see him, either.

"If you're trying to disappear, Beast, you're going to have to find a bigger room to do it in," she recommended. But if the dog didn't want to get in the bath, what was she going to do about it? Beast must weight a hundred and fifty pounds.

She opened the door a crack. "Rob! How do you get Beast into the tub?"

"Just tell him," Robbie advised from the kitchen. "But you have to be firm."

"Terrific," Layne muttered. "Firm is not my best thing." But she put her hands on her hips and ordered, "Get in the bath, Beast."

Beast cowered.

"You look like an abused dog to me, all right. And if you don't get in, I may just beat you," Layne told him. She tugged on his collar, exerting all her strength, and succeeded in getting him six inches closer to the water.

Robbie's head came around the bathroom door. "Beast, get in the bath," he ordered, and Beast rolled his eyes and held out an appealing paw. "Nope," Robbie said, and Beast crawled across the bathroom floor in slow motion and clambered up on to the edge of the bath. He stopped there to give his small master another chance to change his mind.

"Get in," Robbie ordered, and the dog, his tail tucked, splashed awkwardly into the water.

"Thanks, Robbie," Layne said. She hardly believed her eyes.

"You just have to make him believe that you mean it. The shower is the easiest way to get him wet all over, by the way."

"Now you tell me."

"Tony's here. Can we watch TV?"

"If the dishes are done. Is Gary still here?"

"Yeah. He said he'd drink coffee and wait for you to finish with the mutt."

"Marvellous," Layne turned on the shower. The plumbing was baulky today, and the shower, always slow to start, seemed to be on strike.

"Why does he always call Beast a mutt? Hey, don't forget to take off his flea collar. It's still good for a couple of months if it doesn't get wet."

"I couldn't see it under all the hair. Thanks, Robbie. I think we just saved a few dollars." Layne reached for the collar and the shower spit into action, catching her with a full stream of cold water. She fell back, sputtering, and Beast tried to get out of the bath.

After that, the bath was downhill all the way. By the time Beast's coat was lathered, Layne had nearly as much shampoo on her as on the dog, and she kept having to mop water off her face with a towel so she could see. Finally she just turned the shower on and held Beast under the stream, her hands twisted into his long hair to keep him still. He might not have had a complete bath, but it would hold him till Robbie was out of a cast and could do a better job. Besides, she couldn't possible get any wetter; what difference could it make?

She heard a sudden sharp yell from the living room

and jumped, startled. Beast tried to pull away, but when he saw the look in Layne's eyes he subsided under the shower again.

Gary said, from the far side of the bathroom door, "Layne, who do you know who drives a Cadillac?"

"What? I can't hear over the water."

He pushed the door open. "Somebody just pulled into the driveway in a white Caddy, and Robbie took off like a shot."

"A Cadillac?"

"That's what I said."

Beast took advantage of her slackened attention and pulled out of her grip. One leap and he was out of the bath; another and he had brushed past Gary, whose coffee cup went flying, and was down the hall, trailing soapy water. Layne was right behind him.

She turned the corner from hallway into living room less than a yard behind the dog and stopped dead when she saw Robbie at the front door. For standing beside him, one hand on the child's shoulder, was a tall, black-haired man whose blue eyes were dark with cynicism.

"Kyle," she breathed.

He was wearing a light grey suit; his skin, tanned by the summers he had sent on the job sites, was dark against the blindingly white collar of his shirt. The tailored suit showed that he was as slim as he had been that day almost ten years ago when Layne had first laid eyes on him. There were changes, of course, even if they hadn't showed up in the newspaper photograph. There were some new lines in his forehead, as if he found a lot to frown about, and she'd been right about the fleck of white hair at each temple.

But he was just as compellingly attractive as he had ever been. He looked marvellous.

Too bad, Layne thought, that she couldn't say the same for herself. Her hand went automatically to her hair, and encountered a clump of shampoo suds—one of several places Beast had left his mark. One wet brown strand of hair hung in her eyes. Her low-necked knit shirt was soaked. Her sandals squeaked with every movement. She was probably standing in a puddle.

And she remembered the first time she had ever seen Kyle Emerson, the day he had stopped to deliver a message from his father to hers and caught her in her favourite ancient bathrobe recovering from flu. That day he had been fresh from the construction site and had been wearing jeans and a blue work shirt unbuttoned to the waist to bare a darkly tanned chest covered with curly hair. Even hot and undeniably sweaty, he had exuded a sexuality so strong that Layne, innocent as she had been at seventeen, had been rocked nearly off her feet.

Now Kyle was thirty-five, an executive instead of a manual labourer, and driving a Cadillac instead of the Jeep that had been their transportation in the old days.

Facing him today in that elegant suit was nothing like the day of their first meeting. It was infinitely harder, Layne thought. And she realised, with her second thought, that the sexuality that had such an effect on her at seventeen was still there, and just as strong today.

Kyle raised a hand to stroke his tie, and his eyes travelled from her head to her toes, which were wriggling self-consciously in the wet sandals. "Well, Layne..."

What was going to come next, she wondered. I've missed you? How you've grown up? How pretty you are? Whatever it was, it would be patently unbelievable, she thought.

"Layne," he repeated gently, "you haven't changed a bit."

CHAPTER THREE

"How did you find us?" Layne demanded.

Kyle looked her over while he carefully considered his answer. Then he said softly, "I didn't. Robbie found me."

Her eyes dropped to her son, and Robbie shifted uncomfortably on his crutches. "Robert?" she asked.

"You said you didn't want to talk about it, Mom. You didn't say I couldn't do anything. And I'd already done it, anyway." His tone was apologetic, rather than defiant.

Kyle looked down at Robbie with an approving smile, and then turned to Layne. "He called my office yesterday."

No wonder Robbie had looked guilty when she came in last night, Layne remembered. He hadn't been feeling sorry about being hurt, but because he'd just done something that he knew she wouldn't like. And it was a good thing for him that she hadn't known. What would she have done? Strangle him was what she'd like to do now.

"Shall we make ourselves more comfortable and talk about it?" Kyle asked, indicating a chair. "Robbie, I believe this is a matter for the adults in the family. I'll see you again before I leave, and we can make some plans then."

Robbie groaned, but a direct unsmiling look from Kyle silenced his protests.

"Why don't you take Beast to the back yard and hose

the rest of the shampoo out of his coat?'' Layne suggested quietly.

"I'll do it later, Mom." The child let himself out the front door and sat down on the steps, where he could keep an eye on the Cadillac in the driveway.

Gary came in from the hallway, carrying his cup and the towel that he had used to wipe up the spilled coffee. "What a mess, Layne. That mutt of Robbie's should be shot." He stopped as he saw the man in the living room. "Oh. You must be Robbie's father. The resemblance is amazing."

Kyle raised an eyebrow. "And who are you?"

Layne ignored the interruption. "Let's not bother to talk about it, Kyle. I don't think we're likely to come to any amicable arrangement. So you can walk out that door and forget Robbie and me just as you have for the last eight years."

"You have your facts twisted, my dear." Kyle's voice was suave, but underneath there was a thread of steel. "I may have forgotten you, but since I never knew Robbie existed…"

"Layne!" Gary protested. "What's wrong with you? The man wants to take some responsibility for his son. Don't be ridiculous; you're hardly in a position to make any grand gestures."

Kyle looked him over. "You're a man with a practical point of view, I see," he commented. "And your name?"

"Gary Spencer. I'm Robbie's Little League coach."

"It's a bit unusual for a coach to be showing so much concern for an injured player." Kyle didn't actually ask for an explanation, but polite enquiry hung in the air.

You don't owe him anything, Gary, Layne pleaded silently. Don't take the bait.

But Gary did. "I happen to think Robbie is a special kid. And Layne and I are planning to be married," he announced.

Layne put her hand over her eyes.

Kyle's expression did not change. "I do hope that you'll invite me to the wedding," he said politely.

Gary beamed. "See, Layne? I don't know what you've been so afraid of," he said. "We'd be delighted to have you there, Mr Emerson."

Kyle went on as though there had been no comment. "I'd really enjoy watching from the front pew as my wife embarks on bigamy."

Gary sputtered, "What is that supposed to mean?"

"Layne knows," Kyle suggested gently. "Don't you, darling?"

Layne dug her fists into her hips. "Just what makes you think I didn't divorce you long ago?"

"It's very difficult to divorce a man without first serving legal notice that you intend to do so. But you just gave me the proof with that charming, embarrassed little blush. You never could lie worth a darn, Layne."

"You're still married to this character?" Gary's voice was starting to rise.

"Be careful, Spencer. A few minutes ago you were delighted that I planned to take the financial responsibility for Robbie off your hands. Now you're calling me names."

Layne took a deep breath and tried to steady her voice. "I assumed that you had divorced me years ago, Kyle. You had grounds."

"All kinds, as I recall. But it's been an advantage, through the years, to be able to say that I'm still a married man."

"I'm sure it came in handy." Layne's voice dripped

sarcasm; she knew exactly why he hadn't got a divorce, though she had expected that after she'd been gone nearly nine years, he would have given up. "But as much as I'm enjoying this conversation, Kyle, I'm going to bring it to an end. I don't think we have anything to talk about after all."

"I am Robbie's father, Layne."

Layne looked at him with bitterness in her big brown eyes. "Any man can be a father, Kyle. It's a mere biological function, and it gives you no rights."

"It gives me any rights I choose to claim, my dear. We can, however, hardly talk about it here." Those dark blue eyes flicked over Gary, who stood, arms folded, in the middle of the room, obviously unwilling to leave. "Shall we discuss it over dinner? I'll pick you up at seven. Don't dress formally."

"I'm not going anywhere with you, Kyle. I meant it, I have nothing to talk to you about."

"Nothing?" His tone was one of polite interest.

"Nothing." She folded her arms and did her best to look defiant.

He shrugged. "Then I should ask whether you want me to take Robbie with me right now, or if you prefer to have him disappear from your life sometime next week when you least expect it."

"Kidnapping is a federal offence."

"There's been no ruling on who has custody of our son, so you would find it difficult to convince the police that I had kidnapped him."

Layne's voice shook a little. "You'll take him away from me and never let me see him again."

"Don't assume that I'll do what you tried to accomplish, Layne. My mind doesn't happen to work the same way as yours does. And don't try to disappear again.

You couldn't do it this time, and it would make me very angry.'' There was a moment of silence. ''You really should join me for dinner. You might discover that there are some options.''

''And if I don't come?''

''Then you have no options. I'll be back at seven. If you don't plan to have dinner with me, you might as well have Robbie's things packed.'' He pulled a card-case from his pocket and put a business card on the nearest table. ''That number rings directly into my office, just in case anyone wants to talk to me this afternoon. And Layne? If you make Robbie suffer because he called me, you'll pay twice as hard.''

''Kyle! You can't do this to me!''

He raised a questioning eyebrow. ''Is there something special about you? Don't despair, darling. You have all of dinner to change my mind. I'm sure you can come up with something to persuade me. You always used to be able to—if you remember.'' He stopped at the door, one last formality remembered. ''I'm so glad to have met you, Spencer. Layne's taste is very interesting. I wouldn't order the wedding invitations yet, if I were you.''

Layne watched from the window as he bent over Robbie on the front steps, ruffling the child's soft dark hair. Robbie looked up at his father and the expression on his face clutched at her throat. He looked like a child who had just found a Christmas tree surrounded by packages on a hot June morning, when it was least expected.

The two of them walked slowly across the yard to the Cadillac, Robbie swinging along on his crutches, Kyle with his jacket pushed back, hands deep in his trouser pockets, his head bent as he listened to his son's chatter.

Layne watched from behind the curtain as Kyle

opened the car door, then turned back to Robbie to say something. Robbie's face showed disbelief, then he flung himself against his father and tried to smother him in a bear hug. Layne let the curtain drop back into place.

"Why didn't you tell me you weren't divorced, Layne?" Gary asked quietly.

"I didn't know I wasn't. I thought by now he'd probably have got tired of looking for me." She grimaced. "If he ever looked at all," she added in a tone so low Gary couldn't hear.

"What were you going to do? Take it on faith? Cross your fingers all through our wedding?"

"Gary, please don't be sarcastic. I told you last night that I'd never thought about marrying again. It has never made any difference to me whether Kyle had got a divorce. Gary, he wants to take Robbie away from me! And Robbie will go!" Hearing the words seemed to make it even worse. Layne dropped into a chair, her hand across her eyes. "That's what they're talking about out there," she said, her voice low and painful.

"Layne, I'm going home to think things over. I hope you aren't planning to go anywhere with him tonight." He hesitated, waiting for an answer. When none came, he sighed and said, "I'll ask Clare to come over."

She hardly heard him leave, but she did hear Clare at the back door a few minutes later. "Layne? Are you all right? Gary said you needed me." Footsteps sounded across the kitchen tile and then Clare was beside Layne's chair on her knees. "Honey! What's happened? What did Kyle do to you?"

"No more than I expected," Layne said dully. "He said if I wasn't ready to go to dinner with him at seven tonight that I should have Robbie's clothes packed."

It rocked Clare for a second. "In that case, you'd better be waiting for him at seven," she said.

"He's going to take him anyway, Clare. And Robbie wants to go."

Clare sighed. "Do you have coffee made?"

"Unless Gary drank it all."

"Of course he was here to see all this, right?" At Layne's nod, Clare sighed. "Darn Gary anyhow. Let's get you a cup of coffee, and then perhaps you can tell me all about it." She guided Layne to the kitchen, put a box of tissues beside her, and prepared to listen.

Robbie came in a few minutes later. "What's the matter with Mom?" he asked Clare. Without waiting for an answer, he announced his news. "Dad asked if I wanted to come live with him this summer at Wheatlands. What's Wheatlands, Mom?"

"See?" Layne pointed out to Clare, who sighed. "Wheatlands is your dad's house, Robbie."

"I always wanted a house that was important enough to have a name of its own," Clare admitted. "Where is it, anyway?"

"In Mission Hills."

"The most expensive real estate in the Midwest, right?"

"Something like that. Certainly the most expensive suburb of Kansas City."

"What's it like, Mom?" Robbie asked.

Clare intervened. "Your mother just doesn't want to talk about it right now. And whatever came over you to call your father without asking her, anyway?"

"You're the one who said he should be taking care of me."

"I said what?" Clare sounded shocked.

"The other day. The day I broke my ankle. You said

Mom shouldn't have to try so hard when it was Dad who should be taking care of me. Since she wouldn't call him, I did." He sounded half-proud of himself, half-fearful.

"Guilty. Oh, damn," Clare muttered. "Robbie, run along now."

"What did you tell your father, Robbie?" Layne asked quietly. "About staying with him at Wheatlands?"

"I said heck yes. Can I have a cookie, since it looks like lunch is going to be late?" He didn't wait for an answer, just dug a hand into the jar. He stopped at the door to announced, "I'm going to hose Beast off now." Then he was gone, whistling.

"Hard-hearted little brat," Clare muttered.

Layne gave her the first genuine smile of the day. "He only did what you threatened to, Clare."

Clare groaned. "Don't remind me."

"And remember, what happened to him this morning is the biggest event of his life. Imagine, after eight years of knowing only that you had a father, to work up the courage to call him and have him come running as Kyle did."

"He didn't waste any time, did he?"

"Oh, he wasted enough to check it out. I know Kyle that well." Layne reached for a tissue and blotted tears off her cheeks. "I guess I'd better stop this sort of nonsense and figure out what I'm going to do."

"That's one of the things I like about you, Layne. You bounce back. Nothing can keep you down for very long."

"That's flattering, but you're wrong. If Kyle takes Robbie…"

"Surely he won't," Clare said as she reached for the coffeepot. It was empty. "Want me to fix another pot?"

Layne shook her head. "I used the last of the coffee this morning."

Clare gave her an inquisitive look, but didn't question. Layne was grateful. Whether she bought coffee was, after all, a personal decision. It didn't necessarily mean that she was out of money.

"I doubt Kyle will actually ask for custody."

"I agree. I don't think he'll ask for anything," Layne said with wry humour. "He'll just take Robbie."

"But the child needs you. After all, you're the one who has raised him. Oh, Kyle will probably hold you up for visiting rights—summers and holidays like every other divorced father has…"

"You forget. Kyle isn't like every other divorced father. He isn't even divorced."

"But surely…"

"I'm certain he won't stay married for any longer than suits his purpose. And that shouldn't be long now. After all, once he has Robbie he doesn't need me any longer."

"The child isn't some kind of commodity, Layne."

"I'm sure Kyle will learn to love him. No one can resist Robbie's charm. But even if Robbie wasn't a cute kid, Kyle would take him. I'm certain of it."

"So what are you going to do about tonight?"

"I suppose I'll go. He said we'd talk about options, and that if I didn't go, there weren't any options." She thoughtfully sipped her coffee. "I don't suppose it will make any difference, because nobody talks Kyle out of something once he's made up his mind. But—can I borrow your orange dress anyway?"

* * *

It was like getting ready for her first date, Layne thought as she tied the narrow straps of Clare's flame-orange halter dress at the back of her neck. But on her first date there had been anticipation of pleasure. Tonight there was only weariness, and worry, and a deep certain knowledge that no matter what she did or said, the results of tonight's discussion were already determined. Nobody changed Kyle's mind, she had told Clare that morning. And nobody prevented Kyle from doing exactly as he wanted. Except that time, so long ago, when Jessica had interfered with his carefully made plans.

For a moment the bedroom seemed to dissolve around her and she was sitting in the walnut-panelled library at Wheatlands, her fingers tapping on the arm of her chair because she didn't trust her hand not to shake if she tried to pick up her teacup. Sitting there silently as Jessica Tate had told her in that elegant voice of hers just why Kyle had married her.

Layne swallowed hard. That was years ago, she reminded herself, though the pain was as sharp in the pit of her stomach as it had been the day it happened. She sat down at her dressing table and reached for her make-up case, and let herself remember those six long-ago months, the summer she had met Kyle Emerson, and the autumn that she had been his wife.

Layne had grown up in the building trade; her father owned Baxter Construction. Mostly he built one-family houses, but sometimes he would do work subcontracted by other companies. One of the men who called on him often was Stephen Emerson, Kyle's father.

They had worked together so much that year, Layne remembered, that they had even talked about merging their businesses into one. But it had gone no farther than talk; Stephen Emerson ran a conservative ship, while

Robert Baxter would take a flyer on anything. His colleagues had nicknamed him Lucky; they shook their heads pessimistically whenever he made a deal, and shook them again wonderingly when—as usual—Lucky Baxter's bets paid off.

"They'd have fought like cats and dogs over whether to pay the rent," Layne thought with a fond smile. Her father enjoyed sailing close to the wind; he never paid a bill till the day it was due, declaring that there was no sense in letting someone else earn interest on his money. Every penny he controlled he gambled to make another profit. Stephen Emerson was almost the opposite. He had inherited money and by cautious investment tripled his fortune. Working with a partner like Lucky would have driven the careful Stephen into a breakdown in a month.

So the merger plans had come to nothing, and the two men went back to working side by side on a new office building.

And then had come the day that Kyle stopped by the three-bedroom split-level that Lucky had built, and Layne fell in love.

It had ben just about that fast, too, she reminded herself glumly. She had been seventeen and vulnerable, and Kyle had been overwhelming, a girl's dream come true.

What was really unbelievable to her now was that Kyle had seemed to feel the same way about her. In the next weeks he had taken her everywhere—to baseball games, and films at first, and then to dinner with his father at Wheatlands. Layne adored Wheatlands; she felt incredibly clumsy there, but she fell in love with the house as quickly as she had tumbled into love with Kyle.

She'd have gone to bed with him in a minute, but that wasn't what Kyle wanted. "My God, what a gentleman he was," she murmured. She propped her elbows on the glass top of her dressing table and rested her chin on her hands, and remembered one of the arguments they'd had about it.

They'd been sitting in Kyle's Jeep, parked in a secluded lovers' retreat that Layne, in her innocence, would have never known about. And after a particularly long and passionate kiss, Kyle said, his voice husky, "Has anyone ever told you, young lady, that you could set a snowball on fire?"

Layne shook her head and snuggled close to him, but he pushed her gently away. "It's time to take you home," he said.

"Why? It's early."

"Because I've reached my limit, that's why. You don't understand what all your innocent little kitten tricks do to me, and I can't be around you for two minutes without wanting to make love to you."

"Okay."

"Okay, what?"

"I want to make love to you, too, Kyle." She had almost whispered it.

"You don't know what you're talking about. And that's exactly why I'm not going to let you tempt me," he told her firmly. "Your father would kill me. And even more important, you're a virgin, Layne."

"So is everybody, to start with," she told him dryly. "It's no sin."

"But it would be a sin if your first experience was in a Jeep, for God's sake—hurrying so we can get you home on time and with one eye out for anyone who might interrupt and ask inconvenient questions." He shook his head.

"Then what about a motel?" she asked shyly.

He put a finger across her lips. "No. That would make

it feel cheap. The first time I make love to you, we will have all the time in the world. We'll be in our own room, in our own bed. On our wedding night.''

Layne laughed with sheer delight. It was the first time either of them had mentioned marriage.

''You think it's funny that I want to marry you?'' he asked.

''No, I think it's wonderful.''

''All right. I'll talk to your father tomorrow.''

Her eyes widened. ''Kyle, he won't let us. He thinks I'm still a baby.''

''And so you are, at seventeen. But he'll agree to let us get married, I promise.''

It was their first quarrel, and it lasted for an hour, with Layne trying to convince him that the only sensible solution was to elope, and Kyle holding out for a church wedding with the approval of not only her father but his.

Finally he took her home. He kissed her good night, hard, and said, ''All right. If my way doesn't work, then we'll elope.''

Layne clung to him, desolate. ''If your way doesn't work, I'll be locked up in a tower like Rapunzel. Let's run away tonight!''

But he had just laughed and told her not to cut her hair till she heard from him. And the next day he bought Lucky a beer after work, and the two of them came home arm in arm to plan the most lavish wedding ever. She hadn't even set her own wedding date; Kyle and Lucky had already chosen it.

She hadn't known then that her father was dying of a particularly virulent cancer. But Lucky knew, and Kyle's proposal must have seemed providential to him. Married into the Emerson family, Layne would be forever free of financial worries.

"Well, Dad, I'm sure it looked that way from where you stood," Layne mused. "It wasn't your fault that it didn't work out."

She started to apply eyeshadow; it was getting late and she would have to hurry. But the spell of the past was strong, and her tiny brush slowed as she thought about her wedding day.

She had not even had a nervous tremor that day; her bridesmaids refused to believe that a bride could be so calm. But how could any girl who was marrying Kyle Emerson have a doubt in her mind, Layne wondered.

Six bridesmaids had accompanied her down the aisle, walking stiffly to a Bach air; Kyle had chosen the music, Layne the bridesmaids. It had been just about the only thing she had planned about her wedding, she reflected, that and her dress.

The dress was a Southern belle's dream, cut so low in the bodice that Lucky had protested, with puffy short sleeves that left her shoulders bare. The skirt was layers and layers of chiffon edged in ruffles and worn over a hoop, and her veil was a wisp of illusion drifting down from a wide-brimmed hat. Lucky had protested about the price, but one look at his daughter's vibrant face under that outrageous hat and he had surrendered.

"So much fuss about a dress," Layne told her mirror image, a dress that she had left behind without thought when she ran from Wheatlands three months later. She wondered idly what had happened to it. Had Kyle left it tucked in a corner of Wheatlands' attic, as a relic of a mistake? Or had he given it away? It hurt to think that somewhere another girl might have worn her dress, without her knowledge.

"I hope, if that's what happened, that her marriage

was happier than mine,'' she said aloud, without bitterness.

It had started off well enough. Their wedding night had been all that Kyle had promised. He had been so gentle and careful with her initiation that her first fleeting pain was overwhelmed, never to be remembered, by a wave of ecstasy.

She blushed a little even now at the abandon she remembered displaying and the way he had laughed at her eagerness. Of course he had laughed, she realised. There must have been many women who had wanted Kyle as she had. The only thing that had been different about Layne was that she was Lucky Baxter's heir.

Layne opened the bottom drawer of her dressing table and pulled out the framed picture of her father. It was the only thing of value she had taken with her when she left Wheatlands.

She stared at it and remembered how Lucky had cried without shame when they reached the altar and he put her hand into Kyle's, how he had watched with fond pride as her new husband led her on to the dance floor. But the effort drained his strength, and the cancer flashed out again. Three weeks later he was dead.

Layne went into shock. Lucky had been the only constant in her life, and since she didn't remember her mother, she had never suffered a death so close to her. For the next two months she spoke only when spoken to, ate what she was told to, wore whatever was nearest to her when she opened the wardrobe door. She asked once what kind of estate Lucky had left, and Kyle assured her that he would take care of everything. Layne was grateful for his gentle concern, so she stopped thinking about it.

And sometime during those two months, Kyle started seeing Jessica Tate again.

Layne had always known about Jessica; she and Kyle had grown up together. But Jessica had married a wealthy old lawyer, a friend of her father's, and in her innocence Layne believed the blonde beauty was no threat to her. Until that dreadful day when Jessica had ripped away the abstracted cloud in which Layne lived and forced her to face reality.

Layne had been staring out of the library window when the maid showed Jessica in. A flash of feminine feeling was coming back to her; she wasn't going out of her way to look nicer, but she was at least aware of when she looked bad. And that day she looked awful in faded jeans and an old shirt of Kyle's, and a two-months-old haircut.

Jessica, of course, looked like every cent of a million dollars. The little dress was Paris-cut, and her make-up was flawless. She drank her first cup of tea in silence while they waited for Kyle to come home, and Jessica eyed Layne like a cat about to pounce on a parakeet. When the second cup was poured and Kyle hadn't come, Jessica had stirred in a lump of sugar and said, "I hoped that you could take a hint, Layne, but since you can't..."

"A hint about what?"

Jessica eyed her sorrowfully. "You innocent little fool. Don't you know why Kyle married you? Haven't you even read your father's will?"

"No. Why should I? Kyle's the executor."

Jessica looked pathetically surprised. "I am sorry for you, Layne. It must be very difficult, young as you are, to be caught in the middle this way."

Looking back, Layne knew that Jessica's campaign had been planned, but at seventeen she had known only that she had to find out what the woman meant. So she pried until Jessica told her.

The will, Jessica said, had surprised Kyle. He had expected that Layne would inherit the business that had been her father's. But instead, Lucky had played games with his estate, and Baxter Construction would be left in trust for ten years. If there were children born of Layne's marriage in that time, it would belong to them, and remain in Kyle's control, since he was the main trustee. If there were no children, the company would be sold, and the proceeds would go to Lucky's favourite charity.

"Kyle will be a good trustee, of course," Jessica said airily. "And I'm sure you understand now why he refuses to spend a night away from you. If he'd known you weren't going to inherit the business, he'd never have married you at all."

Layne's head was spinning.

Jessica picked up her teacup with delicate grace. "Now that he's gone so far, he hates to give up. But he's hoping that he won't have to wait long for you to produce an heir so this nonsensical marriage can end."

"What is his hurry?" Layne asked dully.

Jessica looked surprised. "So we can be together, of course. Really, Layne, are you that dumb?"

"You're married," Layne managed to croak.

Jessica smiled. "Of course I am, dear. As soon as Kyle is free, I'll get my divorce. I never planned to spend my whole life with Hal; surely you understood that?"

"Why are you telling me all this, Jessica?"

"Because I don't care whether Kyle gets that business or not. I just want him, and I am not going to wait around for you to have a baby." She set her cup down.

''Tell Kyle I'm sorry to have missed him. I'll be seeing you, Layne.''

The will was in his desk. She hated herself for doubting him, hated herself for needing to check on what Jessica had said. But it was all there, detail by detail. If there was a child, Kyle's grip on the company was assured. Baxter Construction would be his then, whether the marriage lasted or not. He would be free to discard Layne and marry Jessica, as soon as their child was born. All he had to do was keep the child.

So Layne packed the few sentimental things she had brought to Wheatlands with her, and left, without a word or a note.

For the one thing Jessica didn't know had made it impossible for her to stay, Jessica didn't know that Layne's doctor had confirmed that very morning that she was pregnant.

CHAPTER FOUR

LAYNE wouldn't have heard the Cadillac whisper into the drive at precisely seven o'clock, but Robbie had been sitting on the front steps watching for more than an hour, and before the car had come to a halt he was standing beside it, waiting for the door to open.

Clare was at the front window. "He's here," she said, and Layne drew a long breath. Somewhere deep inside her there had been a spark of hope that perhaps Kyle hadn't meant it, that perhaps he would not show up.

"You'll be all right," Clare told her. "Just think before you say anything. Try not to make him angry. Now stand up and let me look you over."

Layne obediently stood up and turned a full circle for Clare's inspection. The dark orange dress was like a flame against the peach of her skin, bringing out the gleam of dark brown hair and making the sparkle of tears in the big eyes look mysterious.

"It sounds like you're talking to Robbie," Layne said.

"Well, some days it feels as if you're about the same age. You can do it, Layne."

"Just what magic am I supposed to be able to perform?" Layne asked. "I feel like David going up against Goliath. Except somebody stole my rock."

"Dad's here!" Robbie announced from the door. The grin on his face was the biggest Layne had ever seen. Kyle was beside him, one hand resting lightly on Robbie's shoulder as if to convince himself that the child was real. His eyes swept over Layne.

"I see you're ready to go," he said.

Layne shrugged. "You didn't leave me much of a choice."

Clare's hand clamped down on Layne's wrist. It was all the message she needed to give. Layne bit her tongue. What a way to start if she intended to try to placate the man!

But Kyle apparently hadn't noticed. "Shall we go?" he asked.

Layne reached for the silk shawl that matched the dress. Instantly he was beside her, draping it with exaggerated care across her shoulders. His fingertips brushed across her bare back, and chills straightened Layne's spine.

He felt her shiver beneath his hand, and for an instant they both stood frozen, as if wondering what came next.

Robbie broke the standstill. "Why can't I come?" he asked plaintively. "If you came to see me, Dad, why are you taking Mom out? And why can't I come too?"

"Because you weren't invited," Kyle said easily. "And because your mother and I have a lot of things to talk about. But there will be the rest of the summer for us to be together, Robbie." He tucked Layne's hand into his elbow. "Ready?" he asked.

Robbie trailed them to the car. As Kyle opened the passenger door, Robbie started to protest again, and Layne put a finger across his lips. "Robert," she warned.

"I was only going to tell you that Mr Hamburg is here," he argued.

"Oh, damn." She looked towards the street and saw that Robbie was right.

"Who is this?" Kyle asked. He put her into the car and closed her door.

Layne pushed the switch that rolled the window down. "One of my clients," she said.

Kyle's eyebrows raised. "Just what sort of business do you run here, Layne?" he asked smoothly and walked around the car

"A typing business," she hissed furiously as he slid into the driver's seat. "And though I may not like the man much, he eventually pays his bills." She turned back to the window. "Hello, Mr Hamburg. How are you tonight?"

"I don't suppose you have my last chapters done?" His voice was high-pitched and a bit squeaky.

"Well, no. You did say you were in no hurry, and I have been waiting for your cheque to arrive before I started on the new section."

"Hasn't it come? It must be lost in the mail."

Kyle shifted impatiently in his seat. His fingers hovered over the ignition key. Layne impulsively put her hand over his, trying to still his impatience. The sudden contact was like an electric shock. With an effort she dragged her hand away and focused her attention on Mr Hamburg again.

"I brought that material more than a week ago, Mrs Emerson. However, I suppose it really doesn't matter to you if this book is done on schedule or not, though it most certainly matters to me. There are three publishers waiting to see it."

"I will certainly try to have it done tomorrow." But Robbie goes into hospital tomorrow, the back half of her brain reminded. Well, Mr Hamburg would just have to wait.

"What is really bothering me is that there are three

typing errors in the section you gave me last week. Three!'' He waved an envelope accusingly at her.

And almost a hundred pages, Layne thought rebelliously. "If you'll give the manuscript to Robbie, Mr Hamburg, I'll be happy to correct the errors tomorrow. Be a pet and put it beside the typewriter, would you, Rob?''

Mr Hamburg was adamant. "I'll wait, Mrs Emerson. It will take you just a few minutes. I am, after all, paying for professional service, and you assure me that you are a professional.''

Kyle leaned forward. "I'm sure it has escaped your notice that the lady is going out for the evening,'' he said politely.

Mr Hamburg shrugged. "I'm afraid that's not my problem.''

"It certainly isn't,'' Kyle agreed grimly, and turned the ignition key. The Cadillac's engine purred. "As soon as your cheque gets itself un-lost in the mail, I'm sure Mrs Emerson will do the fastest typing job you've ever seen. So if you want your manuscript, you might start by making sure the money arrives. Personal delivery usually works best.'' He put the car into gear.

Layne didn't know whether to thank him or hit him. The stunned look on Mr Hamburg's face as they drove off was worth a lot; he had bullied her for three months over his manuscript and if she hadn't desperately needed the money she would have cheerfully given the whole mess back with an honest appraisal of its chances of publication. Slim to none, Layne thought. But it was money. What difference did it make to her if she typed trash or literature?

Kyle darted a look at her. "Are you trying to decide whether I did you a good turn or a bad one?''

"Something like that," she said finally. "You've probably lost my steadiest customer for me."

"I shouldn't think so," Kyle said cynically. "You still have a section of his manuscript. He'll be around."

Layne didn't answer. She put her head back against the dark blue leather seat and looked out at Kansas City speeding silently by.

"Why do you work for him, anyway?" The Cadillac slowed and turned on to a freeway ramp.

We must be going over into Kansas for dinner, Layne thought. I hope he isn't taking me to Wheatlands... "I work for him because I need the money," she said finally. "Now isn't that complicated? And don't tell me you didn't have it figured out. I'm sure you know enough about me to fill the Yellow Pages."

"Oh, I wouldn't go quite that far. What does he write? Porno thrillers? Somehow he looks the type."

"No. It's his autobiography, actually. He seems to have been the Don Juan of central Europe during the war."

"Which war?" Kyle asked. "Franco-Prussian? World War One?"

Layne sat up. "Why don't we get to the point of this conversation, Kyle, and quit wasting time? It might even save you the price of dinner because we can probably settle it in five minutes."

"We have to eat somewhere." He didn't sound interested.

"No. *We* don't have to do anything—together, at least. But I do think it would be nice if we could discuss certain things before we bring Robbie into them. For instance, you could have asked me before you invited him to come to Wheatlands for the summer."

Kyle was silent for a few moments, and Layne actually wondered if he had heard. Then he swung the car off the freeway down into city traffic again, and said mildly, "If I had asked you, you would have said no."

"You wouldn't have paid any attention, anyway."

"Probably not. So why bother to ask?"

"Perhaps a better way to put it is that you could have warned me."

"Didn't you expect it? It does seem only fair, Layne. You've had eight summers with Robbie. I'm only asking for one."

"For now," Layne said bitterly. "And when next summer comes…"

The Cadillac nosed silently into a parking space in a huge lot, and Kyle shut it off. Then he turned that devastating smile on her and said, "When next summer comes, I'll take that one too." He held her gaze for a long moment before he came around the car to open her door.

Layne ignored his helping hand and slid out of the car. Kyle was not so easily avoided, however, and before she could slip away he had captured her hand and imprisoned it in the crook of his elbow. He held her firmly against his side, the whole length of her uneasily aware of his nearness.

Halfway across the parking lot he stopped, and Layne was taken by surprise. He didn't say anything for a moment, just stared at the building that lay before them, and for the first time she took a look at her surroundings.

The long, low building was charcoal grey, and it seemed to melt into the landscaped background, the tiered parking lot surrounding it and making it look small. That was deceptive, though, Layne knew, for it took only one glance at the two-storey entrance to recognise that this was North Winds Mall, the largest and newest in the city.

She stole a look up at Kyle, not knowing what expression to expect on his face. Pride? Enjoyment of this achievement? Relief that the project was completed? But she couldn't read his face, and he hesitated only a moment before walking on.

"Robbie will be jealous," she murmured.

"Oh?"

"That I got to see North Winds before he did. He's been reading about it since the day you started excavating."

Kyle stopped and swung her around to face him. He stared down at her with a peculiar expression, and Layne dropped her gaze, unwilling to look directly at him. She wished that she could learn to keep her thoughts to herself.

"Why?" he asked as they walked on.

"What do you mean, why? Because he was interested in you."

"I mean, why did you let him? I have to thank you for that, Layne. You could have poisoned his mind about me. But you didn't." He held the big entrance door for her, his gaze speculative.

Layne didn't trust herself to answer. In truth, she told herself, she didn't know why she had never given Robbie the sort of horrid details that would have made him unwilling to contact his father. And she was paying the price right now, wasn't she? she told herself angrily.

The high-ceilinged entrance was a huge atrium, with fountains splashing musically. Layne would have liked to stop and admire the goldfish, some of them nearly a foot long, that occupied the pools. But Kyle glanced at the big brass clock and said, "We're late now. Felicity's doesn't hold a reservation very long."

Felicity's. Not only the newest, but also the most elegant restaurant in the whole Kansas City area. So much for Kyle telling her not to dress up.

The maitre d' greeted them with a smile and guided them to a table off to the side, probably the best placed one in the entire room for a private conversation, Layne thought. But of course. Kyle had always got that kind of service.

She let the shawl slip off her shoulders on to the back of her chair, glad that she had borrowed Clare's dress. Nothing Layne owned could live up to the atmosphere in Felicity's, but in Clare's dress she could get by. Then she thought, how illogical. Why are you trying to put on a front for Kyle? What do you care?

"Champagne, I think," he was saying to the maitre d'.

"A very appropriate choice," the man murmured, his eyes resting approvingly on Layne. "We have a lovely vintage that I'm sure Madame will enjoy."

Kyle nodded. "Whatever you recommend."

"Why champagne?" Layne's voice was a little breathless.

"Don't you think we should celebrate? Finding each other after nine years… It seems like the proper thing to do."

"Finding Robbie, you mean. It's not as if we're having a reunion, after all." Layne opened her menu.

"That's right," he said thoughtfully. "I did forget to mention it to you."

Kyle had never forgotten anything in his life, Layne thought resentfully. "You forgot to mention what?"

"That Robbie's invitation is extended to you, as well.

I want you to come to Wheatlands with him for the summer.''

Layne's heart jolted. She considered standing up and walking out of Felicity's before this madman's mind turned to axe murder. Why on earth Kyle thought she would ever again set a foot inside Wheatlands was beyond her.

Then she realised her mistake. If she hadn't objected to Robbie's visit, Kyle would never have said anything to her about coming back to the house they had shared in those short months of marriage. It was merely his way of keeping her off balance. And the result would be that she would be forced to agree amicably to Robbie going to live at Wheatlands; if she continued to object, Kyle would merely point out calmly that she was welcome to come too—what on earth was she complaining about?

And once Robbie was at Wheatlands, Layne knew, there was no way Kyle would give him up again. She had been circumvented so neatly that she didn't have an argument left.

Kyle was looking at his menu, so he didn't seem to notice that she had turned pale. ''Let's put off the serious discussion until after dinner. What would you like to eat, Layne?''

There was nothing she felt less like doing than eating, but Lane glanced down at the menu and said the first thing that came into her mind. ''I'll have the lobster tail, please,'' she said. If Kyle was going to play games, she thought rebelliously, he might as well pay the price.

But he didn't even blink as he repeated her order to the waiter and ordered a steak for himself. He handed over the menus, sipped his champagne, and asked, ''What have you been doing for the last nine years, Layne?''

She thought about trying to shock him, then decided that Kyle was probably unshockable. So she told the truth. "The whole list is so long that it would bore you to have to listen. For the last couple of years, I've been a secretary. Not very glamorous."

"Is that where you met what's-his-name? Gary? What does he do?"

"He's a teacher."

"I should have guessed. He's exactly the type. Being a secretary doesn't bring in very good money."

"It's been adequate."

"Why didn't you ask me for an allowance, Layne?"

"You must be joking. I wouldn't take anything from you."

"You took my son from me, my dear," he said softly.

Layne took too large a drink of champagne and had to fight off a sneeze. Then she said, determined that the conversation was not going to slip out of her control, "How is your father, Kyle?"

He was leaning back in his chair, studying her, and for a few moments she thought that he hadn't heard her. "He has good days and bad ones; he is seventy now, you know, and he doesn't get out much. He's delighted, of course, to know that you and Robbie are coming home."

"I haven't agreed to come back to Wheatlands."

"I stand corrected. You haven't—yet." His voice was smooth and undisturbed. "Wheatlands has seemed much too large in the past few years with just the two of us rattling around in it. He always wanted to see it filled with grandchildren."

"What a shame that you didn't divorce me and satisfy his wishes, Kyle." The waiter set a crystal salad plate in front of her, and Layne shook out her napkin. It had been years since she had eaten food like this, and she planned to enjoy it, no matter what Kyle said.

"But now he has his fondest wish, Layne. He's absolutely delighted that we produced a grandson for him to spoil."

It was a veiled way to tell her that Robbie would stay at Wheatlands. Layne didn't bother to answer. She dug into her meal, savouring the mellow softness of the lobster tail.

"It's been a long nine years, hasn't it, Layne? You were still a child when you left Wheatlands. Have there been men in your life?"

"Jealous, Kyle?"

"No. Possessive, perhaps. I never did like to share my toys."

She didn't answer as she concentrated on her dinner, but she was remembering the early days of their marriage, before the magic had been tarnished. It was a little difficult to breathe, she discovered.

When she finally put down her fork with a sigh, he was watching her curiously. "It's been a while since you had one of those, hasn't it?" he asked.

"You probably know to the day how long it's been."

"I certainly know that you prefer lobster to steak," he said mildly.

"You never did like seafood, did you?"

"If God had intended for me to eat fish he wouldn't have arranged for me to be born in Kansas City."

The waiter removed their plates and refilled their coffee cups. "An after-dinner drink? And dessert?" he asked.

Layne shook her head. "I couldn't eat another bite," she told Kyle. "And I prefer to keep my head clear. I've had too much champagne now."

"You sound suspicious of my motives."

"Oh, it isn't only your motives. I'm suspicious of every single hair on your head." A wave of memory swept over her as if she had been tackled, and Layne toyed with her water glass to keep her hand from reaching out to stroke his dark hair. I used to do that whenever I wanted, she thought, and the memory was actually painful.

She picked up her spoon and put too much sugar in her coffee, just to keep her hands busy. "What if Robbie isn't really yours, Kyle?" It was a question almost at random, asked just to see what the answer would be. Was there a shadow of doubt in Kyle's mind?"

"There isn't a judge in the country who would even order a blood test after he took a good look at the three of us, Layne." He saw her expression and spoke before she could say another word? "Do you really think I haven't investigated? I had a busy afternoon, yesterday. I can tell you which hospital Robert Baxter Emerson was born in, on which day of the week, and exactly how many grams he weighed. I even have a copy of his birth certificate. With my name on it, in case you've forgotten putting it there."

"I would have said that, no matter who his father was."

"Layne," he said, "don't try to make yourself look cheap. It isn't going to work. In any case, even if Robbie wasn't my biological son, he would still be legally mine, because you were my wife when he was born."

Layne sipped her coffee. "Is that why you didn't get a divorce?" she asked, keeping her voice carefully steady.

"It would have been an adequate reason, don't you think?" He reached across the table and covered her

hand with his strong tanned one. His voice was gentle.
"I'm going to take my son, Layne. You know I'm not
just saying that, don't you?"

The words branded themselves on her heart, and she
knew as certainly as she had ever known anything that
there was nothing she could say or do to change his
mind.

"Kyle! How unusual to see you here. I thought you
said there were some problems at the office."

Layne looked up, knowing even before she saw the
blonde beauty standing beside their table that Jessica
Tate's path had again crossed hers. Jessica's eyes were
bright with curiosity, and her gaze flicked curiously
across Layne's dress. At least I don't have to be ashamed
of Clare's taste in clothes, Layne thought.

Kyle rose, but didn't let go of Layne's hand. "Hello,
Jessica. You remember my wife, don't you?"

"Of course," Jessica cooed. "How could anyone forget Layne?" The words concealed a dozen meanings.

Layne didn't try to interpret; whatever Jessica had
meant, it was certainly not a compliment. She attempted
to slip her hand out from under Kyle's, but he refused
to let her go.

"I'm glad to see you tonight, Kyle. I found someone
to make the comforter we were talking about for the
master bedroom at Wheatlands, but I can't remember
what you said—did you decide on one of those old quilt
patterns? I think something modern would fit better into
the decorating scheme."

"What about the Wedding Ring?" It was out before
Layne had a chance to consider the wisdom of saying
anything at all.

Jessica looked her over from head to toe. "I see the
child has acquired a tongue in the last few years," she

said icily. "Perhaps you can drop by for breakfast in the morning, Kyle, and we can talk about it in peace. Along with the party we're giving for Governor Howard next month." She glanced pointedly at their hands, still clasped on the table, and swept off.

"Drop by her house, or drop by her bedroom?" Layne asked. "Is she living at Wheatlands?"

"If she was, would I invite her?" His grip on her hand loosened as he settled himself in his chair, and Layne pulled away.

"Probably, if it suited your purpose."

He leaned back in his chair and studied her. Long before his scrutiny was over, Layne was uncomfortable, but she refused to let him know how much it bothered her. Finally he sipped his coffee and observed, "Your fiancé seemed to think that you are afraid of me. Are you, Layne?"

"Gary isn't my fiancé."

"Are you afraid of me?"

"When you talk about taking Robbie, yes."

"But not in any other way?"

"No. Should I be?"

He didn't answer. Instead he flagged the waiter to refill their cups, and when the man was gone Kyle said, "How did Robbie know where to find me?"

"Why don't you ask Robbie?"

"I'm tired of playing games, Layne." Their eyes locked, and Layne gave in first.

She toyed with her spoon. "He saw you on television once and recognised the resemblance right away. He asked if you were his father."

"And you told him?"

"I have never lied to that child, Kyle."

He swirled the remaining champagne in his glass—

evidence, Layne thought, of how agitated he was, for normally Kyle would not have treated a good wine with such disrespect.

"He caught me totally off guard, you know," he said. "My secretary told me it was a personal call, and when I picked it up…"

"Expecting Jessica, no doubt," Layne inserted under her breath.

"This scared little voice asked, 'Are you Kyle Emerson? I'm your son Robbie.' It was incredible, Layne. To know that I have a son—that my father will see his longed-for grandchild after all…"

To see the sudden solution of his problems, to know that he would not have to sacrifice Lucky Baxter's estate to charity after all… It must have been an incredible feeling, Layne thought. "I'd really rather not listen to all the sentimental stuff, Kyle."

He nodded. "Of course not. It can hardly be the sort of thing to touch your tender heart. Are you coming home this summer, Layne?"

"Wheatlands has never been my home. Robbie may come with my permission. I won't fight you any more." She stared into the bottom of her cup as she said it, knowing that she had just signed away her rights to her son.

"What about you?"

"No, thanks. You accomplished what you intended with the invitation."

"I intend that you will come to Wheatlands for the summer."

"Why? You've got what you want. You have Robbie, and even my guarantee not to tear him up over it."

"Leaving you behind will tear him up, too, Layne. Do you want to do what's best for Robbie?"

Layne dropped her spoon in shock. "I don't believe what I'm hearing. You've known the child exists for a grand total of thirty hours, and suddenly you know what's best for Robbie. What makes you the expert parent all of a sudden? Is it a product they sell in stores?"

"I do not intend to have Robbie's adjustment be made harder, as it will be if people are publicly wondering just where he came from, and if he's really legitimate. You will bring him back and live at Wheatlands for the summer."

"Are you asking for a reconciliation? Because if you are, you can just forget it, Kyle. It was over when I left nine years ago."

"Of course it was over. And I don't want to be married to you again any more than you want to be married to me. This is for appearances only, for the summer. On Labor Day weekend we'll announce that our second try at marriage has failed, and that Robbie will be staying with me. By then he'll have settled in and he'll be comfortable at Wheatlands and ready to start attending his new school. And then you can go wherever you want with whomever you want, see Robbie whenever he wants to see you, and have your divorce. I'll even pay alimony."

"My God, your generosity overwhelms me. I can see my son whenever he wants to see me? What about when I want to see him?"

"Take what you can get, Layne. Because if you don't do this, then we'll fight it all the way through the courts—which you can't afford—and we'll follow the letter of the law when the divorce is final. And I'll be more generous with a settlement than the judge will be, I'll guarantee it."

"As if money matters to me. I wouldn't take a filthy dime from you if I was starving!"

He leaned back in his chair. "Layne, what are you fighting about? What are you giving up by coming to Wheatlands for two months? You don't have a job to speak of. If you want to continue your business, I'm sure we can find a place to plug in your typewriter. At the end of the summer you'll have a divorce and alimony, which will make it easier than you've ever had it before."

"And lose my son."

"You'll have had two months with him that you would have missed otherwise. One way or the other, I'm taking him home from the hospital, Layne—home to Wheatlands. You can come there and make it easier on him while he recuperates and enjoy having him to yourself without worrying about where next month's rent is coming from. Or you can fight me and end up hurting Robbie and yourself. If you're not afraid of me, Layne, then just what are you afraid of? Now which is it going to be?"

He was right. There was hurt for her whichever road she took, but if she didn't go with Robbie, he would feel that she had turned her back on him. If she was going to lose Robbie anyway, and she knew Kyle well enough to know that he would not back down, then she did not want Robbie to suffer shame or hurt or embarrassment.

"Damn you, Kyle," she said bitterly.

"Does that mean yes, thank you, I'll come?"

"I'll come. Till Labor Day, correct? And you did say that appearances are your only concern in this reconciliation?"

He raised an eyebrow. "Disappointed, Layne?"

"Hardly."

He didn't appear to have heard. "The appearances had better be good. They'll have to be to convince my father."

"Well, we had everyone convinced that we were made for each other last time, didn't we? I'm sure we can do it again. But perhaps you should let Jessica in on the secret. She didn't look too thrilled at seeing me again, and I'm certain she won't be happy at the prospect of keeping your affair circumspect."

"I'll tell you what I'll do, Layne. Since Jessica obviously bothers you, I'll contract to give her up for the duration."

"No sleeping with Jessica?" Layne didn't quite believe what she had heard.

"None. Of course, there will be no sleeping with Gary either. Fair is fair."

"Don't worry about it. But don't think you're going to substitute me when you get lonely."

Kyle finished off the champagne in his glass and set it down with a thump. "I've lived quite happily for nine years without making love to you, Layne. I think I can hold out for another summer."

CHAPTER FIVE

THE waiting room was quiet except for Kyle's deep, steady voice dictating letters into a miniature tape recorder. Across the room from him was Clare, curled up in a chair and apparently absorbed in her magazine.

Layne stared out the window at the parking lot baking under the July sunshine, listened to Kyle's business correspondence, and thought she would surely go mad.

Two floors below, in surgery, Robbie lay unconscious as they reconstructed his ankle. She really wasn't worried about Robbie, Layne told herself. She was certain that the doctors were taking every possible precaution.

Dr Morgan had been in Robbie's room for only a few minutes this morning, but it had obviously taken just seconds for him to make the connection between Robbie Emerson, orthopaedic surgery patient, and Kyle Emerson, the contractor who had built the hospital. He had looked impressed, and he hadn't made any more remarks about her calling the welfare office. Yes, Layne was certain that Robbie was getting the best of care.

Kyle snapped the recorder off and dropped it into his briefcase. ''You look exhausted today, Layne,'' he commented.

Layne jumped and turned from the window, digging her hands into the deep pockets of the blue sundress. ''Robbie didn't sleep very well,'' she said. ''I'm glad I stayed with him last night. He's never been in a hospital before.''

He looked her over carefully. "Perhaps it's the dress, too," he said. "Blue never was your colour, Layne."

"Thanks, Kyle." Sarcasm dripped from the words. "Sometimes when one is on a limited budget one buys what one can afford, and not what one would like to have." As soon as the words were out, she regretted them. He'd probably think she'd changed her mind about accepting an allowance from him.

He merely raised a dark eyebrow and said mildly, "Even inexpensive clothes come in flattering colours, Layne. Would you like more coffee, Clare?''

Clare hadn't said a word in the last hour. She shook her head, and Kyle got up to refill his cup from the machine.

Layne looked over at her friend. The strain of sitting here was showing on Clare, too. It didn't take an expert to be aware of the tension that hung in the waiting room. It felt like a battle zone.

It had been less than forty-eight hours since their supposed reconciliation had taken place, and the only one on whom the strain wasn't already showing was Robbie. He was delighted at the idea of having two full-time parents. And he was too young even to question why, if they were so anxious to give their marriage another chance, they weren't living in the same house yet.

Layne didn't want to face the idea that as soon as Robbie was released from the hospital, they would go straight to Mission Hills and Wheatlands. It was all too soon, she thought. Perhaps if she had had a few weeks to absorb it, to get herself ready, to prepare Robbie...

When she thought about Robbie, though, Layne couldn't regret that she was going along. She could survive two months at Wheatlands if it made the change easier for Robbie. It would be a tremendous adjustment for him, and he would need all the support she could give him.

He would like Wheatlands, though. The house was a jewel. She had always loved it, from the first day.

"Has Wheatlands changed?" she asked tentatively, hoping to let Kyle see that she wasn't as opposed to going there as she had been—had it been only two days ago that they had talked about it at Felicity's?

"I haven't kept it a shrine to your memory, if that's what you're asking." He wasn't looking at her as he said it, and his tone was casual.

Layne controlled her voice with an effort. "If it hadn't changed at all, it would still hardly be a shrine to my memory. I didn't even move the furniture, if you remember."

Kyle stirred his coffee and returned to his seat. "Perhaps you're right," he said. He looked her over thoughtfully. "I never paid any attention."

I didn't dare, Layne thought, and allowed herself an instant of self-pity. I was too afraid you wouldn't like it, and I couldn't stand it if you disapproved of me.

"You adored Wheatlands just the way it was. Down to the last detail," Kyle mused. "Did you marry me because you wanted to play house at Wheatlands? If so, the charm wore off very quickly."

Clare set her magazine down and groped for her shoes, and Layne shook her head. Don't leave me, Clare, she pleaded with her eyes, and Clare raised her eyebrows and looked even more desperate to escape. But she relented and stayed in the room.

Layne pulled a chair around to face the window and sat down. She didn't answer his question, but she couldn't help giving in to the flood of old memories that swept over her.

She had wanted to change things at Wheatlands. Not major things, just bits and pieces. And she had been afraid to. Wheatlands was so old and so elegant, and she was so young and so inexperienced, that she had been unable to trust her own taste.

Now she was going back, and she would still be the outsider. Obviously Jessica Tate didn't feel the same way, though. If she was helping to choose comforters for the master bedroom...

Layne's chair wasn't comfortable. She perched on the windowsill and watched cars pull into the parking lot. Visiting hours must be officially open, she thought. Robbie was taking a great deal of time down in surgery.

"You've changed, Layne," Kyle added. "You're independent and much more self-assured. You used to be a little mouse who would never say anything until you'd checked it out for approval."

For your approval, she thought sadly; it had always been the most important, Layne swung around from the window. "What did you see in that little mouse that made you marry me, Kyle?" Would he tell her the truth? She braced herself against the window ledge. Perhaps it would be better to have it out in the open, she thought, than to go on this way.

Kyle sipped his coffee and set the cup aside. "I don't remember," he said flatly, and opened his briefcase with a snap.

Layne looked over at Clare, who rolled her eyes. Layne almost started to laugh.

Illogically, she was relieved. He didn't want to hurt her by detailing the truth, she thought. Then she started to wonder. Did he realise that she already knew the answer to her question? Had Jessica bragged of what she had done that day at Wheatlands?

It was another half hour before he looked up again. "Would you stop pacing that floor?" he demanded.

Layne stopped in the centre of the shiny tiles. "Which floor would you prefer me to pace? It's taking too long. He should have been back up here by now."

"They don't allow anyone in the recovery area, so Robbie will be back in his own room by the time they call us. It take a little time."

She turned her back on him again.

"You really care about him, don't you, Layne?"

"Of course I do. He's my son."

"He's mine, too. So why don't you think I care about him?"

He seemed to know that she would not answer. He picked up his briefcase. "I'll be back in a few minutes. I'm going to go make some telephone calls."

As soon as he was gone, Clare uncurled from her chair and stretched. "Layne, it's driving me crazy to sit here and watch him take potshots at you. Just how in heaven's name do you expect to live through two months of it?"

"I don't plan to spend much time in the same room with him, that's how. Clare, you're a darling to stay here."

"It seems as if Robbie is taking forever."

"I know. How do people stand these places, anyway? And this is only minor surgery. How do parents make it through their child's open-heart surgery, or something serious?"

"You do what you have to do," Clare said, and shrugged her shoulders. "The human animal is amazing. And I suppose that's how you can make it through the summer, too. Are you going to keep your house, so you can move back to it in the autumn?''

"No. I called the landlord last night and told him. There's no point to it; Robbie won't be coming back with me and I don't need the house if I don't have a boy and a dog—an apartment will be plenty." Layne's voice was cheerfully determined.

Clare looked as if she didn't believe a word of it. "Is Kyle going to let him keep Beast?''

"I think making him leave the dog would be the only thing Kyle could do that might give Robbie second thoughts. And Kyle was smart enough not to do it. Beast moves to Wheatlands with us.''

"Now that is coming up in the world, for a stray sheepdog to end up in Mission Hills.''

"Beast will love it. The social level of cats is much higher, and he'll soon discover that it's a lot more fun to tree a registered Persian than an ordinary calico. Nobody calls the fire department to rescue the calico.''

Clare laughed. Then she said, "You're all right as long as he's not around, aren't you? Kyle, I mean.''

Layne nodded, ''I doubt he'll be there much. He used to work fearful hours, and I can't imagine that he'll have relaxed that. So when he's gone, I'll have Robbie. And when Kyle gets home, I'll retreat into the wardrobe until he leaves, so I don't interfere with his time with Robbie.''

"It all sounds so fearfully cold.''

"Of course it is, Clare. Neither one of us wants to do this, but we do have to watch out for Robbie, and he won't be helped by a battle between us or by losing contact with me.''

"I can't imagine that he'll be helped much by seeing this farce of a marriage, either.''

"It's better than the alternative." Layne swung her foot, deciding that she had to buy shoes soon. There was nothing left on her wardrobe floor fit to wear. "Didn't you say Gary would stop by?"

"Yes, but he had something to do first. Can't remember what it was." She saw Layne studying her shoe, and said, "We need to go shopping, Layne. You can't go out there with the clothes you've got."

Layne shook her head. "I can't afford to buy more, and I won't spend a dime. I have little enough hoarded as it is, to get me through the summer."

"Won't Kyle give you an allowance?"

"He's suggested it. But I don't want to owe him a cent. Even if it's actually my father's memory that he gives me, Kyle will expect something in return. I have my pride, Clare."

"I know," Clare sighed.

"And if he doesn't like the way I look, he can just put up with it. It won't hurt him to suffer a little aggravation. What good would a Mission Hills wardrobe do me two months from now?"

"Plenty, when you go back to work. He's right, you know. Even inexpensive clothes come in flattering colours, and that blue was a mistake."

Layne held up a fold of the skirt as if inspecting it for the first time. "Robbie liked it."

"So let's make him a shirt out of it." Clare looked up as Gary came in. "It's about time," she told him.

"Sorry. Why is it always the mornings I'm in a hurry that everything runs late?" he mused. He rested his folded arms along the back of Layne's chair. "We need to have a talk, Layne," he said, and nuzzled the nape of her neck.

"About what?" Layne asked. She sat up straight, uncomfortably shifting away from his touch. She hadn't seen him since he had left her house, declaring that he had some things to think about. She wondered what conclusions he had come to.

"About us," he said. He sounded a little surprised.

Clare glanced at her watch and reached for her shoes. "I really have to be going," she said. "Give my love to Robbie—I will see him again, won't I?"

"I'm not sure, Clare. We won't be coming back to the house, but you can always come and visit us."

Clare nodded and brushed her lips against Layne's cheek. "I'll be thinking about you." Her heels clicked away down the hall.

Gary asked, frowning, "What do you mean, you won't be coming back?"

"Didn't Clare tell you?" But obviously she hadn't. "Robbie and I are going to Wheatlands as soon as he's released from the hospital."

"What?" Gary almost screamed the word. "You're going back to live with that man?"

"Not exactly," Layne parried. "It's only for the summer."

"Oh, just a brief fling, right?" He paced across the room. "Layne, I love you, but I can't put up with any more of these games."

"I'm not playing games. Kyle is going to take Robbie to live at Wheatlands whether I go or not. And it will be a lot easier on Robbie if he has me to rely on until he gets used to his new surroundings."

Gary shook his head. "I should have expected it. After all, what am I, beside Kyle Emerson?" His voice was heavy with sarcasm.

"It's got nothing to do with Kyle! I'm only going because of Robbie."

"I don't believe what I'm hearing. You swore that your marriage was over. You even let me believe that you were divorced and done with him. Then as soon as he snaps his fingers you're right back in line to get into his bed. Well, Layne..."

"I am not going to be in his bed!" Layne was furious. "Gary, I've made no promises to you. Right now my son is the most important thing in my life. I will do whatever Robbie needs. And he needs me to be at Wheatlands this summer."

Gary just shook his head. Finally, he said softly, "You're lying, Layne. To me, and I think even to yourself. I'm not staying around for any more of it." He didn't look back.

At the door, he brushed past Kyle, muttering something under his breath. Kyle's eyebrows drew together, and for a split second Layne wondered if he was going to put his fist through Gary's face. But the instant passed so quickly that she told herself she had imagined it.

She sat frozen in her chair. Kyle regarded her thoughtfully as he retrieved his cup and refilled it. He sat down across from her, still watching her over the rim of the cup. Finally he said, "Volatile, isn't he? I suppose you told him that you wouldn't be sleeping with him this summer. Didn't he take it very well?"

Layne looked up. "For your information, Kyle, I haven't been sleeping with Gary," she snapped.

"Oh? It certainly didn't look that way to me. The first morning I came to your house he was in the bedroom when I arrived. Was he just getting up, or was he waiting for you to come back to bed?"

"He wasn't in the bedroom! He..." What was the use, she asked herself. Kyle had made up his mind and he would believe as he chose. He certainly wouldn't believe the story about Beast and the coffee cup—at least not until he knew the dog better.

"Poor Layne," he mused. "Your love affairs never have gone smoothly, have they? Tell me, have there been many men in your life? And have they all been like Gary?" The tone of his voice suggested that, if so, there was something remarkably wrong with her.

Layne was still groping for words when a young nurse came to the door of the waiting room. "Mr and Mrs Emerson? Robbie is back in his room now. He's still very sleepy, but he'd like you to come in."

Robbie talked nonstop from the hospital to Mission Hills, chattering about everything from the prettiest nurses on the paediatric floor to his speculations about how Beast would like the new neighbourhood.

He didn't say anything about his own feelings, but Layne could hear uncertainty dragging along under the flow of words. And she was glad all over again that she had agreed to come. What would Robbie have done, she wondered, if she wasn't in the front seat of the Cadillac?

She stole a look from under her lashes at Kyle, who was devoting most of his attention to the freeway. Traffic was heavy this morning, and he was negotiating it carefully. But he looked happy, she thought, and now and then he smiled at Robbie's chatter. It was a smile she remembered from the early days—indulgent, fond. She wondered if he had felt fatherly towards her, too. It wouldn't surprise her if he had.

The Cadillac left the freeway. The houses they were passing were large, set well back from the streets on big lots. It was a neighbourhood of professionals, Layne thought; a doctor or a lawyer in every four-bedroom ranch. They were twice as large as the tract houses Robbie was used to, and in nearly every driveway was a motorcycle or a van or a boat.

"Is Wheatlands like this, Dad?" Robbie questioned eagerly.

A teasing smile played over Kyle's face. "Not quite, son."

"Oh," Robbie looked a bit disappointed, then returned to eagerly inspecting each house they passed.

"Kyle, are you being fair?" Layne asked softly. It hadn't occurred to her to warn Robbie about the house they were going to; she had assumed that Kyle had told him all about Wheatlands.

He shrugged. "I hadn't considered whether it's fair. I do know it will be fun to see his face when he first sees the house."

Layne let it drop. It was a little late to warn Robbie now.

"Did you do anything about my furniture and car?" she asked. Kyle had dismissed the whole mess with a wave of his hand and announced that a crew of Emco's employees would take care of everything she had left behind.

"Yes. The furniture is in storage till you need it in the autumn, and the dog is at Wheatlands. The car went directly to the repair shop, however. The man who drove it didn't like the way the brakes felt."

"I won't have a car to drive?" The brakes had been fine the last time she drove it, Layne thought. And it had just been in the repair garage a few weeks ago. Surely they would have noticed...

"Only for a little while. It shouldn't take long, even if it requires a complete brake job."

"Wait a minute! I can't afford to put new brakes on The Tank. I realise it isn't much of a car, but it is mine.

And it's paid for, unless I have to mortgage it so I can afford the repairs.''

He looked over at her for a moment, frowning. ''I would say that you can't afford not to repair the brakes. But you may consider it my treat.''

''That sign said Mission Hills,'' Robbie announced from the back seat.

''Indeed it did, Rob. You're almost home.'' Kyle smiled at him in the mirror.

''I don't want any favours from you,'' Layne said stiffly.

''And I don't want you driving an unsafe car, so it's going to be checked over from headlights to muffler.''

''When will I have it back?''

''When the garage had pronounced it totally safe to drive.''

''But…'' To be stranded in Mission Hills, miles from anywhere, without transportation, was an invitation to mental illness.

''Mom! Look at the houses!'' Robbie's tone was rapt. He had obviously not heard a word of the exchange in the front seat.

Layne had always thought Mission Hills was one of the most beautiful residential areas in the country. Every urban area had its stately homes, but usually they were in a small district. Mission Hills, however, was an entire town of lovely old mansions. Many of the families, Kyle's included, had lived in these houses for generations. Wheatlands had been built by Kyle's grandfather, after he had amassed a fortune from the wheat farms in western Kansas.

Kyle turned the Cadillac on to a winding street and pulled up to the kerb. ''Robbie,'' he said, ''that's Wheatlands.''

The child craned his neck for the best possible view of his new home, and when she saw the look on his face, Layne had to turn away. It was easier to look at the house than it was to watch the delight play across Robbie's face. His eyes held something akin to recognition, she thought. Robbie was a true Emerson. Wheatlands was in his blood.

She looked across a little valley to where an enormous red brick house stood proudly on the hillside, its stone trim gleaming in the late-morning sunshine. Tall bay windows jutted out from the façade on the first and second floors. On one end of the house, above the entranceway that could shelter a car while its passengers got out, there was an open porch, and on the other end were two closed-in sun rooms, one above the other. Ivy crept up one wall, its huge waxy leaves shading some of the lower floor windows. Several chimneys peeked over the steep roof.

"We're going to live there?" Robbie breathed. "Oh, Mom!"

"For as long as you like," Kyle told him. And his eyes, meeting Layne's, reminded her that her invitation was good only until the first week of September.

He released the brake and the car rolled quietly forward, down the little slope and then up to the big house. It was scarcely stopped before Robbie—cast, crutches and all—had flung himself out of the car.

But it seemed that, once on the grounds of Wheatlands, he didn't know what to do. For there he stood, just staring up at the house, silent and looking so small and uncertain that Layne's heart ached.

Kyle shut the engine off and came around to open her door. "My father will be waiting to have lunch with us," he said. "He's anxious to meet Robbie."

It was all she could do to force herself out of the car. On the front steps, she froze, unable to move another inch. She stared at the heavy front door with its intricate carving and wished that she could just close her eyes and vanish.

Kyle turned at the door to watch her hesitation. "If you'd like, I could carry you over the threshold," he said finally.

Layne's face flushed as she remembered their wedding day, when he had carried her into Wheatlands to be greeted by applause from the household staff waiting in the front hall. "No, thanks," she said tartly. Her indignation gave her strength, and she patted Robbie's shoulder and stepped through the doorway to face Stephen Emerson.

The hall was dim, and after the sunlit outdoors it took an instant for her eyes to adjust. In that moment, a rich, deep voice said, "You're prettier than ever, Layne. And this must be my grandson."

It startled Layne, for the voice seemed to come from somewhere near her left elbow. She jumped and turned, and then had to look down. Kyle's father was sitting in a wheelchair, his hands folded in his lap. It shocked her; Kyle had said nothing about his father being an invalid, and the Stephen Emerson she remembered had been active and healthy.

"Hello, sir," she said.

Stephen frowned. "Layne, I thought we agreed years ago that if you couldn't manage Dad, you'd call me Stephen," he scolded.

Layne said, "Yes, sir," caught herself, and smiled. This old man had been a good friend to her father, despite their many differences of opinion. She had always felt that he wanted to be close to her, but something had kept her from confiding in him. Perhaps it had just been that, after losing Lucky, she had been unwilling to risk letting anyone else take his place.

"That will be enough of that, my dear," he said. Then his gaze slid, as if caught by a magnet, to the child beside her. "So this is Robbie," he murmured, and cleared his throat. Layne wasn't surprised; she was fighting off tears herself. "Come here, child."

Robbie, uncharacteristically quiet, hopped over beside the chair.

"Quite a pair, aren't we?" Stephen said, pointing first to Robbie's crutches, then to his own wheelchair. "I guess we'll just have to be invalids together this summer."

"Yes, sir," Robbie said uncertainly.

Stephen smiled. "Do you know, Robbie, I've been waiting to read *Treasure Island* again, but it seems a foolish thing for a seventy-year-old man to do. But if you'll be kind enough to listen, I can pretend that I'm doing it for your benefit."

Robbie giggled. "Yes, sir."

Kyle glanced at his watch. "Lunch is waiting," he commented.

"I'll take Robbie to wash," Layne volunteered, suddenly anxious to be by herself for a few minutes.

"I just had a bath," Robbie protested, but he swung down the hall at her side.

She found the small powder room easily enough; it was in the same place, but it had been redecorated. Jessica Tate's work? she wondered as she stood in the hallway, staring out over the acre of lawn through heavily leaded casement windows as she waited for Robbie to wash his face and hands.

He came back with ears almost gleaming. "How did you know where to go, Mom?"

Layne ruffled his hair. "I thought you knew that I lived here a long time ago. Before you were born."

He thought about it, then asked the question that she had always known would come someday. "Why did you leave?"

"We'll talk about that when we have more time," Layne said steadily. "But they're waiting for us in the dining room, and I think on our first day here..."

Robbie never missed a meal if he could help it. "Okay. Why is he in a wheelchair?"

"I don't know. Your father didn't tell me about that."

"Can I ask him?"

"I don't see why not. But I think you should wait till you're alone with him, and not pester him at lunch. And Robbie?"

"Yeah?"

"Lunch at Wheatlands is going to be a little different than it is at home. So..."

"I'll mind my manners."

"Thank you, Robbie. And I think after lunch a nap would be in order for you."

"Mom! I'm not a baby," Robbie protested.

"Of course not. But you did have surgery just a couple of days ago. Remember?"

"Mother..."

A maid uniformed in powder blue with a white cap and apron was waiting for them near the dining room. "Lunch will be served in the solarium, Ma'am," she said. "If you'll follow me?"

"That won't be necessary," Layne told her gently. "I can find my way."

The girl nodded and disappeared down the hall. Robbie craned his neck to see where she had gone. "Was that a maid, Mom?" he asked in a stage whisper.

"Yes, Robbie," Layne said dryly and tugged him towards the solarium. The first week will be the hardest, she told herself. After that, he'll be an old pro at this.

The solarium windows were open, and a gentle breeze was sweeping over the glass-topped table, set casually for five. Four wicker chairs were drawn up to the round table, as was Stephen Emerson's wheelchair. Across the room, staring moodily out over the grounds, stood Kyle, arms folded across his chest.

And next to him, hand on his arm and whispering fiercely into his ear, was Jessica Tate.

Kyle turned at the sound of Robbie's voice and came quickly across the room. He always had beautiful manners, Layne thought. Even though there is nothing he wants less to do than touch me, he will not violate the gentleman's code—a lady must not seat herself without assistance.

He held her chair, then let his hands rest casually on her shoulders for a moment while he answered a question of Robbie's. Layne tensed under his touch, and his hands tightened warningly. She caught a twinkle in Stephen's eyes as he watched them, and knew with sudden anger that Kyle had planned it. Kyle had never been public with demonstrations of his affection; his hands so casually possessive of her would be far more convincing to his father than the most passionate of kisses. Layne told herself that she was glad that a possessive touch would be all she had to suffer.

He seated Jessica next to himself, while Layne was almost opposite him. And the blonde's red-tipped fingers only left his arm when it was necessary to pick up her spoon. Why was she here, anyway, Layne wondered. Had she invited herself? Or perhaps Kyle was doing a balancing act, indicating to his father that all was well between husband and wife, but also taking this quick way of making sure Layne knew that he didn't intend to give up Jessica. In any case, Layne decided, she didn't care. She'd do her best to be a lady, and Jessica could do as she liked.

"Jessica, I'd like you to meet my son Robbie," Kyle told her as he shook out his napkin. "Robbie, this is Miss Tate."

"Oh, please call me Aunt Jessica. After all, I'm a very close friend of your father's." Her eyes were hard as she studied the child. Then she turned to Layne. "He certainly looks like Kyle, doesn't he? How...fortunate for you."

Robbie looked up at Layne, sensitive to the tone of Jessica's voice but not understanding why she sounded angry.

Layne patted his knee under the table, and Robbie relaxed and dug into his soup.

He was across the table from his grandfather, who seemed to be unable to take his eyes off the child. "I don't know, Jessica," Stephen said finally. "I think the person he looks most like is Kyle's mother, actually. She was a true beauty, with the heart-shaped face and that same unusual colouring. Kyle has a lot of me, but Robbie is a boyish version of his grandmother." He looked steadily at Jessica as he finished, and she muttered something unintelligible and stared at her plate.

What a perfect way to put her in her place, Layne thought. With one quick comparison, Stephen had made it plain not only that there was not a shred of doubt about who Robbie's father was, but that the subject wasn't to be raised again. Bless your heart, she thought, and hoped that she and Stephen could work on developing that friendship they had only begun all those years ago.

"Marvellous soup, isn't it?" Stephen asked her. His eyes twinkled as he savoured a bite with exaggerated gusto. "Mrs Andrews is an excellent cook."

Layne laughed with a suddenly lighter heart. Perhaps, she thought, this isn't going to be so impossible after all.

CHAPTER SIX

BY THE time lunch was over, Robbie's eyelids were drooping, and Layne could see the ferocious struggle he was making to stay awake.

Stephen saw it, too, and before Layne had a chance to suggest a nap, he said, "It looks to me as if it's time for us to retire for a siesta, Robbie." He yawned. Layne wasn't quite sure if it was pretended or not.

"Do you take naps too?" Robbie asked.

"Every day. Just coming down for lunch makes me tired."

"Does it really?" Robbie looked a little doubtful.

Jessica looked disgusted. It was a fleeting expression, and Layne just happened to be looking her way, or she'd have missed it. But Kyle had seen it, too, she noticed, and he looked disappointed in Jessica. Well, of course he was, Layne thought, and decided that if she was a true lady, she'd warn Jessica that the surest way to Kyle Emerson's heart right now lay directly through his small son.

But there are limits to being a lady, she concluded. Then she nearly dropped her fork as she realised for the first time that Jessica Tate would very likely be Robbie's stepmother.

The poor child, she thought, and was again glad that she had come to Wheatlands. At least this way, when she left Robbie could call her or see her anytime he wanted, and she could help him adjust to the rough times. If she hadn't come, Kyle would never have let her see him again.

Stephen pushed his chair back from the table. "Are you going to the office today?" he asked Kyle.

Kyle shook his head. "I'm going to shut myself in my study and catch up on my paperwork."

"Then perhaps you'd like to come with me," Stephen told Layne. "We have a few years to catch up on."

"I thought you were going to take a nap," Robbie accused.

"Layne's review of the last few years will probably put him to sleep," Jessica murmured. "Kyle, you will have a few minutes for me, won't you?" She tucked one hand confidingly into his arm and gestured prettily with the other. "I need to talk to you about the governor's visit. It's only a month away, you know, and Cam deserves the very best party we can put on." Her voice trailed off as they left the room.

Kyle had not said a word directly to Layne all through lunch. She tried to dismiss it from her mind, but it wouldn't go away. He was the one who wanted this to look good, she thought, and then to pull a stunt like that in the first hour she was in the house...

Their pace was slow, allowing for the purr of the motorised wheelchair and Robbie's less-than-enthusiastic progress. "It's a slower life than the one you're used to, Layne," Stephen commented as he pushed the button to summon a tiny elevator.

Robbie was delighted, and in the midst of his questions Layne didn't have to respond. On the second floor, Stephen turned his chair to the right. It made scarcely any noise on the carpeting. Layne glanced at the floor and realised that this was all different from what she remembered. The hall carpet had been a deep pile; now it was all tightly woven and flat to give the least trouble to the wheelchair. The downstairs halls had been like that too, she realised. So Stephen's confinement to the chair was neither a new thing nor a temporary one, if Kyle had recarpeted what had always seemed to her to be miles of hallway.

"Here is your room, my dear," the old man said, drawing the chair to a silent halt outside a closed door.

"Things have changed at Wheatlands," she said lightly. "It was your room before."

"Yes. But the new arrangement is much more practical for me. I'm at the other end of the hall, in the last room." He gestured. "It opens on to the sun porch, and now that it's so inconvenient for me to go outside, the porch is my most precious possession." He turned the chair. "Robbie will be right across the hall from you, Layne. I hope you'll come down to see me after he's settled."

"I will." There were plenty of questions she'd like to ask, she thought. Though she didn't know if Stephen would answer them.

Robbie's room looked out over the huge lawn. From this angle, it looked as if Wheatlands stood alone, instead of being surrounded by other houses discreetly tucked into the hills.

It was obvious to Layne that the room had been redecorated just for Robbie. She certainly didn't remember it having blue plaid wallpaper and a set of bunk beds. Kyle hadn't wasted any time in producing a young boy's heaven.

Robbie was exploring feverishly. "Mom, all my clothes are here."

"Of course, dear. The maids unpacked for you. That

does not mean, however, that you no longer have to pick up your things.''

''That's what I was afraid of,'' Robbie grinned. ''And two window seats! I've always wanted one, but to have two…'' He sat down on one of them. ''Where's Beast?''

''I don't know.'' Layne had forgotten the dog. ''I expected him to come bounding up when we arrived. But your father said he's here, so after your nap, you may go look for him.''

''I'm not sleepy now,'' Robbie announced.

Layne put her hands on her hips. ''Robert, there's the bed. No more arguments.''

Robbie gave in. ''Can I use the top bunk?''

''Can you get up and down the ladder with your cast?'' She watched as he demonstrated. ''Why did I even ask? Have a good rest, Robbie. I'll come back to check on you later.''

He kicked off his shoe and it bounced on the blue carpet. ''Oh, I wish I could stretch my other toes,'' he complained. ''This cast itches already.''

''Be patient, honey. Maybe in a couple of weeks you'll have a walking cast, and then the crutches can go.''

''I can't wait.'' But his voice was already dragging with sleep.

She found Stephen on the enclosed sun porch, looking out over the wide lawn. A young man was with him, arranging water jug, glass and the latest bestseller on a table beside the wheelchair.

''I'm sorry,'' Layne said, ''I didn't mean to interrupt.''

Stephen laughed. ''Come in, Layne. This is Dave, my keeper.''

The young man looked up with a smile. ''He's exaggerating, of course, Mrs Emerson. I'm just a nurse, actually.''

"Listen to him, saying he's just a nurse," Stephen said sadly. "That's why I've titled him a keeper. It's actually a term of respect. He keeps me under control, keeps me sane…" He looked up at Layne and gestured towards a chair. "Dave, Mrs Emerson will sit with me for a while. Won't you, dear?"

"I'll be in my room if you need anything," Dave said and quietly let himself out.

Layne watched as Stephen carefully shifted himself in the wheelchair, obviously with a great deal of pain. "Kyle didn't tell me that you had been ill."

"Kyle refuses to believe that I might never get better," Stephen said. "Oh, he's faced reality enough to replace the carpet and build ramps and install the elevator, but he still doesn't believe that a little thing like arthritis could keep me in a wheelchair. My son has a great deal of faith in me."

"It's rheumatoid arthritis?"

"Yes. I had to get the nasty kind. And I didn't help matters along. Work has always been a cure-all for me, Layne. When I had the flu, I sweated it out on the job site. When I had a headache, work was my aspirin. When Kyle's mother died, I drowned my depression in my business. So when my doctor told me I had arthritis and to slow down and rest, I laughed at him, and worked all the harder. It wasn't a masculine thing to do, to take naps. So—here I am."

"It must be very difficult for you."

He smiled. "I've learned to accept it. There are still things I can do, and I must be grateful for those. If I can no longer be with the men when they lay the last steel beam at the top of a building, then crying about it won't change it. The one it's really hard on is Kyle. He hates seeing me tied to this chair.''

Yes, Layne thought, Kyle would hate that. He never sat still for an instant, and neither had his father—in the old days. "I thought arthritis patients all moved to Arizona," she said lightly.

"I considered it. But my rheumatologist thought the stress of the move would be even worse for me. Of course I'd have had to go alone, because Kyle certainly can't move Emco. So I stay here."

"Is there any hopes for improvement?"

"Some delaying tactics, at least. They gave me new hips last spring. In the autumn, after I've fully recovered from that surgery, they'll replace my knee joints. The doctors hope that I'll be able to walk then, but I'll have to borrow Robbie's crutches, no doubt.''

Layne smiled. "I'm sure Robbie will be delighted to be rid of them."

"Can't say that I blame him. He's a beautiful boy, Layne. His manners are unusual in so young a child.''

"Well—if I were you I'd reserve judgment. When the new wears off, he may be a bit difficult. But I've tried to raise him the way Kyle would have wanted." Now what had made her say that? It certainly hadn't been in her mind.

Stephen looked at her closely, and Layne dropped her eyes and suddenly became very interested in the design in her skirt fabric.

Then he said gently, "I wouldn't worry about Jessica, my dear. She was an adolescent passion of Kyle's, no more than that. But now that you're back..."

Now that I'm back—what? Layne wondered. Obviously Stephen's love for Kyle was of the blind variety, if he couldn't see that Jessica Tate was not exactly a passing fancy.

"Why is she calling herself Miss Tate now?" Layne asked.

"Oh, it's just a little affectation she's picked up lately. Hal died several years ago. She wore black for months."

"Only because she looks charming in black, I'm sure."

Stephen smiled but didn't answer.

"I thought perhaps she'd got a divorce. When did she start the boutiques?"

"Not till after he died. She said he hadn't left her very well off, and she had to turn a profit somehow." Stephen shrugged. "I find Jessica a bore."

"What's this about the governor?" she asked. "Didn't she say he was going to visit?"

"Part of his next campaign, I suppose. To a politician, there is always an election year coming, and Cameron Howard was born a politician. He's been leaning on Kyle to help draft legislation for greater safety in the building trade."

"I didn't know Kyle was interested in politics."

"He isn't, and it's a good thing, because after Kyle has done the work, Cam Howard will present it as his own brain child. But Kyle doesn't seem to mind. He's only interested in results, he says." Stephen tried to hide a yawn. "And Jessica is interested in Cam. I think she'd like to be the First Lady of the State, if she could persuade Cam to see it the same way."

Another bit of a self-deception? Layne jumped up. "You need your rest, Stephen, and I feel a little worn out too," she said. "I've spent the last couple of nights with Robbie in the hospital, and it isn't the most restful place to sleep. Shall I call Dave for you?"

"No need." He indicated the small electric bell at his elbow. "You're right, of course; I do need my rest. There will be all kinds of time for us to talk. Please stop by my room, Layne. I get lonely up here."

Suddenly touched, she leaned over him and dropped a kiss on his forehead. "I will," she promised.

"I'd like to have Robbie join me for some of his meals, by the way," Stephen added. "I usually have a breakfast tray, and then come down for lunch, but I don't like to eat dinner as late as Kyle does. I keep nursery hours up here. It would probably be more to Robbie's taste than waiting till eight o'clock."

Layne laughed. "Yes, Robbie likes his meals on time. I think he'd love to join you."

"And you and Kyle will want to have your evenings to yourselves, anyway."

That was a prospect that hadn't occurred to Layne. Two months of evenings alone with Kyle... Then she shrugged it off. He'd figure out a way to avoid it, she knew. And she could do her part, too. She wondered where he had put her typewriter, and if he would let her rearrange one of the extra bedrooms so she could have a place to work.

She peeked into a few of the rooms. Most of them were obviously unused, with curtains drawn to shut out the hot summer sunlight. But all were kept scrupulously clean, and they could be ready for a guest at a moment's notice.

"It would be wiser not to explore, Layne," she muttered to herself. She might stumble on to something she'd rather not know about—a stock of Jessica's lingerie, for instance. But she doubted that Kyle would flaunt his romance in front of his father; there were much easier ways to carry on an intrigue. And at any rate, she thought, if Jessica was leaving clothes at Wheatlands, Layne knew which room they would be in. The corner one. Kyle's room.

The one that had been hers, as well as his. She stopped outside the big corner bedroom, staring at the closed door. Did he still have that huge antique bed where they had snuggled together on those cool autumn mornings— the bed where Robbie had been conceived? She put a hand to her flushed cheek and shook her head at her own foolishness.

What difference did a room make, after all? Any room would change in nine years, and Kyle had probably set out to change it as much as possible. Layne told herself firmly that it would be a relief to walk into that room and realise that it was nothing like it had been when she left. It would help to put to rest some of those old ghosts.

But she couldn't force herself to open the door. Instead, she smiled ruefully, shook her head, and walked back down the hall to the room Stephen had showed her. Someday soon, perhaps, she could go into that other room. But not today.

Her bedroom was large and airy and cool. Lightweight curtains were drawn against the strong afternoon sun. On the dressing table was a milk glass vase containing a dozen yellow roses, their heavy perfume scenting the air, droplets of water still clinging to the delicate petals. She leaned over them and took a deep breath. Someone had been very thoughtful. Or had Kyle just been doing what was expected of him?

The card peeked out between the flowers, and she tugged at it. ''Welcome home, my daughter,'' it said.

''It was sweet of Stephen to remember how much I like yellow roses,'' Layne told herself loud. Why should she care that the flowers hadn't come from Kyle? She wanted no complications in this impossible situation. She wanted nothing at all from Kyle.

A row of doors along one wall concealed all the wardrobe space a woman could want, she knew, but Layne couldn't work up the enthusiasm to look inside. It would, after all, be only her own clothes hanging there. She wished for a moment that she had taken Clare's advice and the last of her money and gone on a shopping spree. Perhaps she'd feel a little less like a poor mouse next to Jessica Tate.

Then she shook her head. "Face it, Layne," she told herself firmly. "You will always feel like a poor mouse next to her. Because you are. And don't let yourself forget it. If you do, Kyle will remind you that you are no competition."

The big bed was mahogany, rubbed to a gleam, with canopy and side curtains of a tiny blue and brown print on an ivory background. It was a restful print, and the bed looked so comfortable that Layne kicked off her shoes and tossed herself down. At least in sleep, she reminded herself, she could forget.

"Mom?" a small, plaintive voice asked. "Mom, aren't you ever going to wake up?"

Layne struggled up through the depths of sleep. "Robbie, go away," she said faintly.

"You're going to sleep through dinner."

"Good." But she opened her eyes. "I thought I told you to take a nap."

"I did. A two-hour nap. But you've been asleep even longer than that." His tone was offended. How could anyone who wasn't forced actually sleep in the middle of the day, Robbie seemed to be asking. He sat down on the edge of the canopied bed and, forgetting his disappointment with her, plunged into a one-side conversation.

Resigned, Layne plumped up her pillow and propped herself against the headboard.

"There's a swimming pool, Mom! Out behind the house. A great big swimming pool. If I put my cast in a plastic bag..."

"No, Robbie. No swimming with a cast on."

"Can I ask the doctor?"

"Yes, as long as you promise to stay out of the pool in the meantime."

"Okay. And there's a bike path. And Dad said he'd teach me to play golf at his country club as soon as the cast comes off. He said I can even use the clubs he had when he was a kid."

"That's a switch. It's not like him to be cheap," Layne muttered.

"And there are some great climbing trees. Big ones! Wait till Tony comes to visit."

"Wait till the cast comes off." She'd recited the phrase a hundred times, and she was tired of hearing it, but someone had to remind Robbie that he did face some limitations.

But Robbie seemed not to have heard. "There's one that could hold a big treehouse. I've always wanted a treehouse, but all we've ever had is little trees."

"I think you'd better take that up with your father before you start construction. Did you find Beast?"

Robbie's face fell. "Yeah. He's out behind the house. He's got a pen and a run, but..."

A first-class kennel, Layne interpreted. That made sense; a run-of-the-mill doghouse would not fit into the architectural style of the community. "But?" she prompted.

"He can't come in the house. Why not, Mom? He never broke anything in our old house."

"I wouldn't exactly say he never did," Layne parried. "And Wheatlands isn't quite the same as our old house, Robbie."

"But Dad said I could keep him…" Tears were starting to form in Robbie's eyes.

Layne wanted to go downstairs to Kyle's study and take him apart. Robbie's dog was terribly important to him; couldn't Kyle understand that Beast was not just a pet? Then she sighed. Her intervention would do no good; if she tried, Kyle would be only more adamant.

"Perhaps he doesn't realise how strongly you feel about Beast," she said gently. "If you tell him about it…"

Robbie dashed the tears out of his eyes. "Then will Dad let Beast come in?"

"He might. But even if he doesn't, you'll have done everything you can."

Robbie's face was still sad.

Layne ruffled his hair. "The fresh air will do Beast good," she said. "And you, too, when you go to see him."

"But who's going to walk him? He needs exercise."

"We'll walk him," Layne promised.

Robbie rubbed his eyes. "Is this a mansion?" he asked suddenly.

"Yes, I think you could call Wheatlands a mansion." Layne glanced at the mantel clock and pushed herself up off the bed. Time to be getting ready for dinner, even if she would rather plead exhaustion or a slight case of leprosy and stay in bed. If there was one thing she didn't feel ready for, it was dinner with Kyle. She wondered if Jessica would be there, or if she'd be on her own. "It's about time to get ready for dinner, Robbie. I think you should dress up tonight.''

"I already had dinner with Grandpa.''

Well, Layne thought, that was progress. From "sir" to "Grandpa" in six hours.

"And he doesn't make me change clothes," Robbie added with a touch of defiance.

"I'm sure that's much more comfortable for you. I'm going to go take a shower, Rob. I'll be back in a few minutes if you want to stay and talk to me while I get ready.''

She was still in the bathroom, just pulling Clare's orange dress over her head, when Robbie said from the other side of the door, "And what good is a mansion, anyway, if I can't even have my dog?''

Layne refused to get excited. "You still have the dog. He just isn't sleeping on your bed any more." She came out of the bathroom, tugging at the zipper. "Rob, would you help me get this zipped?''

The door opened and Kyle came in. "Did everybody have a good nap?" he asked no one in particular, and started to unbutton his shirt.

Layne was too stunned to move.

Robbie had no such qualms. "Dad!" he cried and flung himself on Kyle, who wrestled the child to the floor and tickled him.

"Unfair!" Robbie declared. "I'm handicapped.''

"I know. That's why I'm doing it now." Kyle got up and tossed his shirt over the arm of a chair. Then he seemed to see Layne for the first time. "Shall I zip your dress?''

Ever the polite gentleman, she thought. He ever asks permission. She turned round obediently, and suffered in silence the gentle brush of his fingers up her spine as he closed the zipper.

"You wore this when we went to Felicity's," he said.

"Congratulations. You may go to the head of the class."

"Don't you own anything else? Or is it just your favourite?"

Layne looked at him steadily. "Yes, it is my favourite, primarily because I don't own anything else. As a matter of fact, I wouldn't have this one, but Clare decided it looked better on me than it did on her, after she loaned it to me that evening."

Kyle grunted. "She's right, you know. She's too blonde to carry off flaming orange. It looks a lot better on you, with those big brown eyes."

"I'm glad to see that something about me has your approval. I might warn you that you may get tired of seeing this dress by the first week of September."

"So buy some new clothes. Charge them to me." He didn't sound interested.

"I am deeply appreciative, Kyle." Sarcasm dripped from her voice. "But no, thank you. I'll wear what I have."

He shrugged. "Suit yourself. If you want to be an uncomfortable little dumpling, go right ahead."

"Speaking of being uncomfortable—this is making me very nervous. What are you doing here?"

Kyle raised an eyebrow. "I live here," he pointed out.

"Would you stop being purposely obtuse?" Layne asked, her teeth gritted. "What are you doing in this room?"

"I already told you. I live here." He pulled open one of the long row of closet doors and took out a dark blue bathrobe.

"Oh." Layne's head was swimming and her voice was small and shocked. "But your father said this was my... My clothes are in..."

"Of course he did. And of course they are. It is still customary for a husband and wife to share a room, Layne." He disappeared into the bathroom.

Not this husband and wife, Layne thought. And as soon as he comes out of that bathroom I'll tell him so. She saw Robbie sitting on the corner of the bed watching her with unbounded interest. "Why don't you go visit Beast?" she suggested. "He must be lonely."

"I want to talk to Dad about him."

"Later, Robbie. Your father has things on his mind." Or he will have as soon as I get through with him, she told herself.

"Oh, Mom..." But he dragged himself towards the door.

Layne was waiting for Kyle when he got out of the shower. She was sitting at the dressing table with a lipstick brush in her hand. "I assumed you still used the corner room," she said stiffly.

He seemed surprised to see her there. He pulled the belt of his bathrobe tighter and briskly towelled his hair while he considered her comment. Then he shrugged. "Lots of things change in nine years, Layne."

"Are you moving your things out, or shall I move mine?" she asked.

"Nobody is moving anything. Just how long do you think it would take for my father to hear that we aren't sharing a room?"

"Why don't we try it and find out?"

"Look, Layne, nothing is going to happen."

"You're darned right nothing will—because one of us is moving out."

Kyle came across the room and stood behind her, holding her gaze in the big mirror above the dressing table. "Layne, if you attempt to move into another bedroom, you'll find your possessions on the front lawn."

"Sleeping on the grass would be better than sharing that bed with you!"

He tossed the towel down on the foot of the bed, and his hands rested gently on her shoulders. Though he was putting no pressure on her, she could feel the raw strength in his fingers. He could bruise her without effort, she knew, though he had never touched her in anger. The only bruises he had left on her were those unintended ones of passion...

"Funny," he mused. "You didn't think that way before. You were always eager to make love with me." His hands slid gently down over her bare shoulders and cupped her breasts. His hands were warm through the thin fabric of the halter top.

"Would you take your hands off me?" she said, trying to keep her voice from shaking.

"No, I don't believe I will," Kyle said thoughtfully. "You never used to flinch away from me when I touched you. Now if I take your arm or hold your chair or even brush past you, you pull away from me."

"You're not exactly holding my chair right now," she said. Her voice seemed to catch in her throat.

"Has someone taken over your lessons where I left off, Layne? Is that why don't want me to touch you? I can't believe that you aren't still as passionate as you ever were. Who is he, Layne? Gary?"

She shook her head, but Kyle didn't seem to notice. "He hardly seems the type. But then you didn't either, at first. A tomboy from head to toe. Who would have expected you to be capable of melting a man's bones?"

A curious shiver ran through her, like an electric current, and she knew that whatever else had happened to her in the last nine years, the fatal attraction that Kyle Emerson had always held for her was still there.

His hands wandered over her body, and he said, "It was so much fun to teach you about yourself, Layne—to hear you pleading in my arms and in my bed—"

If he wanted her now, she could not stop him. Her own body was betraying her, she knew, but she couldn't prevent herself from leaning against him, from turning her head to brush her cheek against the soft hair on his arm, from wanting to throw her arms around him and beg him to make love to her as he used to do. Jessica was forgotten, and the nine years past might have never been. If she could have Kyle's passion, she thought, she didn't care if she didn't have his love...

He pulled away from her suddenly, and Layne swayed on the bench. She held on to the edge of the dressing table with both hands, fighting the dizziness, not knowing why he had let her go, but grateful that he had. How can you do this, Layne, she asked herself. How can you let yourself get so far out of control? And what was it she had told Gary? She'd assured him that she wasn't about to go to bed with Kyle, that was sure. And here she was, within inches of doing exactly that.

It's only a physical attraction, Layne, she told herself, nothing more. Just a physical desire for a man you once cared about.

"Don't try your tricks, Layne," he said, picking up his towel. "You can't pull it off any more. It's a single-edged sword now, and you'll only hurt yourself and tempt me to punish you. How unfortunate for you that we had nothing more than an unusual compatibility in bed."

She stood up suddenly. "I don't have to listen to this."

"What's the matter, Layne? Angry that the old methods don't work any more?" And as she stepped across the threshold to the hallway, he added, "There's a couch in the sitting room next door. Use it. But don't fool yourself into thinking you're any safer there than in this bed."

CHAPTER SEVEN

CLARE was weeding the flowerbeds by her front door when Layne parked the compact station wagon in the driveway. she looked up, startled, and then got to her feet with what must have been, Layne thought, the expression she turned on door-to-door salesmen. Layne gathered up her handbag and Robbie's letter to Tony and got out of the car.

Clare looked stunned. "Darling! I certainly didn't expect it to be you in the new car. Where have you been hiding yourself?"

"It's only been three weeks. And I've called you a dozen times, Clare."

"It feels like forever." On the lawn next door—Layne's old lawn—two little girls squealed as they splashed each other with a hose. From the front door, a sharp-voiced woman told them to quit it. Clare rolled her eyes and said, "That's part of why it feels like forever since you left. Let's go in—the coffee's hot. How's Robbie?"

"He's fine. He didn't come because he and Kyle are building a treehouse today, but he sent Tony a letter."

Clare dropped her gardening hat and gloves on the counter and handed Layne a mug. "And I'll bet it's going to be the best treehouse west of the Mississippi."

"You're probably right. They've been through the whole process—blueprints and all. Kyle isn't wasting the opportunity to show Robbie how exciting it is to build things.''

"Are you still bitter?'' Clare asked quietly.

Layne sipped the coffee. ''No. I've hauled Robbie out of that tree three times in the last week. At least this way he'll have a ladder so he's less likely to break the cast.''

"I was talking about Kyle.''

Layne sighed. ''I think I'm over the worst of the bitterness. He will always be Kyle, and no one is going to change that. He doesn't plan to be a bulldozer—he just can't help it.

"I see you're driving a new car.'' Clare hunted for her pack of cigarettes on the kitchen counter. ''Is it Kyle's?''

"No, I won the Irish sweepstakes,'' Layne said tartly. "Of course it's Kyle's. He says The Tank has unsafe brakes and needs a muffler and must have the rust removed and who knows what else. Every time I ask him when will it be finished he tells me something else that's wrong with it.''

"Well—The Tank was a rolling disaster area, Layne.''

"Oh, all of it is probably true, of course. But I think the real truth is that it would injure Kyle's image to have me driving around Mission Hills in The Tank. And it was confirmed when I searched the glove compartment of this car today.''

Clare lit a cigarette and inhaled deeply. ''So what did you find, Layne?''

"He told me it had been sitting in the garage for months—that he bought it to use at the construction sites but ended up using the Cadillac instead because it was always handy.'' She raised her cup and said over the rim of it, "But the sales slip was in the glove compartment. It says he bought the car two weeks ago."

Clare shrugged. "Sounds like a pretty thoughtful guy to me."

Layne's eyes got even bigger. "If you'd like to have him, I'd be delighted to put him under your Christmas tree."

"I don't think I could get by with it," Clare mused. She got up to refill her coffee cup. "So how is life at Wheatlands?"

"Jessica Tate is underfoot constantly, the cook has a bad case of impudence, Beast has been banished to the back yard, Robbie is threatening to break into Kyle's workshop and saw off his cast, Kyle is his usual warm and charming self, and I'm going nuts. Would you like me to elaborate?"

"You can start with the last one. You look as if you haven't had a decent night's sleep in two weeks."

"I haven't." The couch in the sitting room was hard and narrow, and frequently she arose in the morning feeling no more rested than she had been the night before. But as long as the alternative was the room next door, she'd stay on the couch if it killed her, she vowed.

"Well, you look awful."

"Thanks." Layne looked longingly at Clare's cigarette, and then caught herself. She didn't even smoke, and that thing looked good.

"Are you going to last the whole summer like this, Layne?"

"Only five weeks left now. And of course I'll last. If for no other reason, I'll do it just to prove to Kyle that he can't drive me out. He's the one who put the Labor Day limit on this thing."

Clare sighed. "I hate it when you sound so cynical."

"I don't much like myself these days, either. I needed to talk to someone who would tell me it isn't all my fault. I feel so out of place at Wheatlands, Clare. The cook is planning to retire on what she's stolen from the household money, and even if I could prove it, I can't do anything. It's not my place to fire the help."

"Can't you tell Kyle?"

"Kyle isn't speaking to me. On the whole, it makes things easier."

"What are you arguing about now?"

"It may have something to do with the fact that I'm still refusing to take an allowance." Layne refilled her coffee cup.

"Oh, Layne, you're hopeless sometimes. Why not let him give you something? It's no more than paying you for the job you're doing."

"Kyle said that, too. But I'm not paid to be Robbie's mother."

"No, but if you weren't there he'd have to hire a nursemaid. Just what are you gaining by arguing with him?"

"A lot of satisfaction."

Clare just folded her arms and looked at her friend. "Heaven knows you need a new wardrobe. That sundress you're wearing looks worse on you every time I see it."

"Clare, I just don't want to owe him anything. Not one cent."

"Are you still going to get a divorce?"

Layne was speechless for an instant. Then she gestured with her cup. "Look, Clare, this is not a fairy tale we're talking about. It's more like a soap opera."

"Isn't all this squabbling making it hard on Robbie?"

"Oh, we don't squabble. We are all three very pleasant to each other at breakfast. Then Kyle goes to work, and Robbie and I do as we like. We have lunch with his grandfather, nap in the afternoon, and get everything cleared up by six so Kyle doesn't have to know what we've been up to. Then Robbie has dinner with Grandpa, and Kyle and I conduct a cool, civilised conversation through cocktail hour and dinner and up until time to put Robbie to bed. Then, after he's tucked in, we're free to fight. Lately we haven't even done that. Kyle goes to his study to catch up on all of his work and I shut myself in my little corner with Mr Hamburg's fascinating life story.''

''Are you still typing that?''

''In spurts. It gives me a little pocket money, when he pays me. And it may be the biggest epic of all time; he's only up to the Normandy invasion.''

Clare shook her head. ''Robbie must know what's going on.''

''He knows that he's better off than he was, if that's what you mean. There's nothing Kyle wouldn't do for that child. He's been to every Royals home game. And since Robbie missed the Fourth of July because he was in hospital, Kyle declared a special celebration a week late. He bought rockets and flares and whatever all those fancy explosives are called. They went miles out into the country and had their own holiday.''

Clare didn't argue. ''Did you say Beast is banished?''

''Um-hum. He's got a doghouse straight out of *Architectural Digest*—probably the only one Emco will ever build. But he's not allowed inside Wheatlands. Kyle has a point, too, Beast may be housetrained, but he's not exactly mansion-broken.''

''And that has Robbie upset.''

''That's an understatement.''

"How is his ankle?"

"It's healing nicely. In another few days we can get rid of the crutches—they'll put him in a walking cast. Dr Morgan is putting it off because Robbie organised the entire junior population of Mission Hills into a crutches race."

"I don't quite understand."

"It was an obstacle course. And Robbie won the race. That was what disillusioned Dr Morgan." Layne drained her cup. "And then there's Jessica. Kyle may not be sleeping with her—that would certainly account for the evil looks she's been giving me lately—but she's spending hours and hours at Wheatlands. I think she's conspiring with the cook. And if that sounds paranoid, let me tell you this. If I wasn't a little paranoid by now, I'd be crazy."

"Who am I to argue with that kind of logic?" Clare murmured.

"Then there's Kyle's father, who tells me—or Kyle or both of us—at least once a day that he'd be delighted to baby-sit so we can have a second honeymoon. Yesterday he suggested Acapulco. I fully expect that by next week he'll be bribing us with Hong Kong."

"Perhaps he's only trying to heal things, Layne."

"Why can't everyone just let me bleed in peace? How's Gary?"

"Haven't you heard from him? He's over here all the time mourning for you."

"I thought perhaps he'd written me off forever."

"Is that what you want him to do?"

"Of course not. Gary is a good friend, and I'm not always going to be at Wheatlands." Layne looked at her watch. "I must go. I have to stop and talk to the caterer and the florist. The governor is coming to town next week, and the Emersons are entertaining him at Wheatlands.''

''But that's an honour, Layne!''

''I could live without it. Especially since it was Jessica's idea in the first place. She planned it to be Mr Emerson and Miss Tate who threw the party, you see.''

''And you feel that Kyle is using you.''

''How'd you guess?'' Then Layne's cynicism softened. ''I have put off doing anything until it isn't possible to put it off any longer. In fact, I'll be lucky if I can still get a caterer. I may end up assembling cucumber sandwiches myself. At least I wouldn't have to be charming to the guests, that way,'' she added thoughtfully.

''If you need help...''

''Oh, I'm sure someone will take us. After all, Wheatlands and Governor Howard thrown in together is any caterer's dream come true.''

''I wish I could do more for you. You look so unhappy, Layne.''

''Keep trying to straighten me out. Why don't you come out to Wheatlands in the next couple of days? Kyle's going to be gone—he has a shopping centre site up in Minneapolis to check into. As a matter of fact, I'm taking him to the airport tonight, so I know we'll be safe. Bring Tony. I guarantee he'll like the treehouse.''

''We'll try, Layne.'' Clare waved goodbye as Layne backed the car out of the drive.

It did feel good to be driving the new car, she admitted as she cut through Kansas City traffic. The scent of a new car was unlike any other aroma, and this little beauty was a pleasure to drive. It had been in the garage for a week while she struggled with her conscience. If she refused to take Kyle's money, how could she justify driving a car he provided? But necessity had prevailed. Obviously he wasn't going to allow The Tank to come out of the repair garage before Labor Day, and she could hardly spend the entire summer inside Wheatlands. So she had given in quietly, hoping that he wouldn't comment.

She detoured to sneak a look at one of Kyle's new projects, a forty-storey office building in the heart of the downtown area. Robbie had been out to all of the construction sites with his father, but Layne had not been invited to join them. It had hurt when she first realised that Kyle wanted her to have nothing to do with his business. But at least he couldn't stop her from driving by.

The walls were going up quickly and twenty storeys of bronze-coloured glass already hung from the steel skeleton, reflecting the buildings of another age that surrounded it. The beauty of the glossy exterior brought a tightness to her throat. She had grown up in the building trade herself, after all, and she knew the joy of watching a building grow. How proud her father would have been that his company had a part in constructing such a piece of art. And she had no doubt that the building would be exactly that.

She admired it from the street, wishing that she dared to walk up to the construction boss and ask for a hard hat and a tour. But Kyle would find out, and he would not like it. So she drove on by.

As she had suspected, the caterer was wildly enthusiastic about the prospect of a garden party at Wheatlands, and he babbled on about liver paté and watercress sandwiches and champagne until Layne's head was aching. The florist was equally excited, and it took a while to convince him that she wanted only daisies for the garden party. He finally gave in, with a wave of his hand. "If that is what Madam wants," he said, with a total lack of enthusiasm.

"It is exactly what Madam wants," Layne assured him. "Now for the house itself, for the dinner party…"

He was instantly alight with charm. "For Madam, red roses," he interrupted, and Layne started to think seriously of choosing another florist.

Errands done, she turned the little station wagon towards Wheatlands. She wondered if the treehouse was completed. Robbie had been pestering for the last ten days, but Kyle had made him plan and sketch and draw blueprints… It was good experience for Robbie, Layne knew, even if it did wear his patience thin.

And Kyle was good with the child. Robbie adored him, and Layne's one big fear, that Kyle would not discipline his son, was proving unfounded. In fact, instead of becoming the little brat that Layne had feared he would, Robbie was thriving on Kyle's attention. And if Layne felt a little left out and unnecessary now and then—well, that was to be expected, wasn't it? She had to keep reminding herself that in five more weeks she wouldn't be there at all, for Robbie to depend on.

She parked the station wagon next to Kyle's Cadillac and looked down across the lawn to the big tree. There was no activity, and from this distance, it looked as if little had changed since she had left hours before. Perhaps the construction was going slower than planned. Or perhaps the chief worker had gone on strike and demanded a lemonade and cookie break, Layne speculated.

Stephen's car was drawn up next to the back entrance, motor running. As Layne crossed the courtyard, the young male nurse brought the wheelchair down the ramp.

"Going for an outing?" Layne asked as she opened the car door.

Stephen didn't answer till, with David's help, he had painfully transferred himself from chair to car. Then he looked up at Layne with a smile. "Some outing," he said. "I get to visit my doctor. And if I'm very, very good, David promised me an ice-cream cone."

Layne patted his cheek. "Sarcasm does not suit you, Stephen."

They drove off and Layne entered the house, trying not to worry about Stephen. He'd been in severe pain the last few days, she knew, though he seldom said anything about it. But if it was bad enough that he was willing to see his doctor, it must be even worse than she had suspected.

The kitchen was cool and quiet, only the hum of the two large refrigerators interrupting the silence. The cook was at the sink, snapping fresh green beans. She looked up as Layne came in. She didn't say a word, but her eyes were frosty, as though questioning why this intruder was in her kitchen.

And intruder was what Layne felt like, too. She supposed it was natural that Mrs Andrews resented her; for years her kitchen had been her own and no one had interfered in her orders. Now this upstart of a young woman was asking questions about her suppliers and wanting to look at the menus.

What was it about Mrs Andrews that bothered her, Layne asked herself. The food was good; the woman definitely had talent. But there was a rigidity about her, a lack of willingness to bend... Perhaps that was all it was. Robbie certainly didn't like her, but then Robbie was used to rummaging through the refrigerator whenever he wanted a snack. Layne couldn't blame Mrs Andrews for not approving of that.

And then of course there was her suspicion that Mrs Andrews was getting kickbacks from the grocers. But Layne pushed that to the back of her mind. It was only suspicion, after all, and she had no power to demand the receipts. That was Kyle's business, and Kyle could not have cared less.

"I'd like you to suggest a dinner menu for the evening that Governor Howard will be there," she said. "There will be eighteen for dinner."

Mrs Andrews' fingers didn't pause, and for a few moments Layne wondered if the woman had even heard. Then she looked up from the green beans again. "Whatever Madam wants," she murmured with faint insolence. "And Mrs Emerson? Please tell your little boy that my kitchen is not a restaurant. I am not a short-order cook, and I do not make fresh lemonade and chocolate cookies just because he expresses a desire for a snack."

Layne counted to ten. "Since this house now contains a small boy, Mrs Andrews, I suggest that keeping the cookie jar full is a new part of your duties. If you don't wish to assume it, then give Robbie an apron. He is quite capable of making his own."

Someday, she thought as she left the kitchen, I am going to lose my temper with that woman. And then Kyle will probably be furious.

The doorbell pealed just then, and the little blue-uniformed maid came running past her to answer it.

Layne arrived in the front hall at the same instant as Kyle and Robbie came down the stairs. Kyle was dressed in light blue trousers and a navy shirt, his jacket draped over one arm, and he was carrying a tooled-leather briefcase. He looked upset and angry, and when he saw her waiting at the foot of the steps his eyes narrowed even more.

Layne glanced at her watch and breathed a sigh of relief. She wasn't late; they had plenty of time to get to the airport. So it must be something else he was angry about. And the fact that she was wearing her blue sundress again wouldn't help at all.

Robbie was trailing his father down the stairs, and as Layne watched he suddenly raised a fist and rubbed tears out of his eyes. Her heart melted. Poor little guy, she thought. His dad is leaving him, and he's scared.

At the front door, the maid said, "But, sir, if you'll wait here, I'll tell Mrs Emerson you want to see her..."

"I'll tell her myself." It was an impatient voice with a guttural accent."

"Mr Hamburg," Layne murmured, as the little man appeared from the foyer. "Just what we needed to improve Kyle's mood."

Mr Hamburg shook a finger as he crossed the hallway to the foot of the steps. "Young lady, I don't know what you think I'm paying you for, but it seems to me I'd be better off to mail my handwritten copy than to wait any longer for you to finish that typing. Now that you've moved into a fancy house it seems to me you just don't care what kind of work you do. And you're purposely trying to increase the number of pages so I have to pay you more."

Kyle reached the bottom step, and said, "What seems to be the problem?"

"Would you just mind your own business, Kyle?" Layne turned her back on him. "What makes you think I'm cheating you, Mr Hamburg?"

He waved a sheaf of paper at her. "Just look at these pages! Look at the number of half-empty lines!"

"That's where you started new paragraphs, Mr Hamburg," Layne protested automatically.

He ignored her. "And you still expect me to pay fifty cents a page for this kind of work? Well, I won't do it!"

Kyle reached for the typed sheets and flipped through them. Then he pushed them back into Mr Hamburg's hands. "I wouldn't pay fifty cents a page for them, either," he commented cooly.

"Kyle! That's a fair price, and you know it!"

Kyle ignored her interruption. "I'd find myself another typist, Mr Hamburg—one who understands how to work with a professional person like you. Now you just write Mrs Emerson a cheque for what she's already done…" He glanced enquiringly at Layne.

She said faintly, "The balance right now is twenty dollars. But, Kyle…"

"I'll pay you ten. In cash," Mr Hamburg announced, and thrust a bill at Layne."

"But…"

"Take it, Layne." It was an order, and Layne accepted the ten-dollar bill. She tried to argue, but everything was happening so quickly that she couldn't get the words to come out.

"And I certainly hope, Mr Emerson, that you can keep her from cheating anyone else as she has me. She shouldn't be in business!" The little man nodded his head briskly for emphasis.

"I couldn't agree with you more," Kyle said grimly. "You have the entire manuscript, now?"

"Oh, yes. I made sure of that before I came. She hasn't got anything of mine left."

"Good," Kyle told Mr Hamburg, and steered him towards the door. "I'll certainly try to keep her under control."

Layne thought about bursting into tears, but she was too angry. When Kyle came back into the hall, she said, "Twenty dollars was a fair price, Kyle."

"No, it wasn't. Fifty cents a page to decipher his handwriting—you should have charged him five times that." He pulled tow bills from his wallet and crumped them into her hand. "Here is the rest of what he owes you."

"I won't take money from you!"

"It's a bribe to get rid of me. And believe me, Layne, it's cheap!"

She wadded the bills up and threw them at him. She would have told him exactly what she thought of him, but Robbie was still there, sitting in a corner of the stairway with his chin propped in his hands. So she stormed up the steps instead.

She was halfway up when she heard Robbie burst out suddenly, "We could at least go look for him, Dad."

"I don't have time, Rob." Kyle's voice was firm.

"You don't even care that he's gone!" Robbie accused.

Layne started back down the stairs. "Who's missing, Rob?"

Robbie met her halfway and flung his arms around her. "Beast ran away because *he* was mean to him." There was a note of contempt in the childish voice.

"Robert, that isn't true," Kyle countered. "You let the dog out of the kennel, and you didn't keep a close enough eye on him."

"Beast ran away?" Layne pushed an unruly lock of hair back out of Robbie's eyes. "How long has he been gone?"

"Most of the afternoon," Kyle told her. "Rob let him

out while we were working on the treehouse and forgot about him. The dog will come back when he's ready.''

"But he doesn't know his way!" Robbie cried. "He's been locked up in that kennel all the time, and he doesn't know his way back. He never ran away at home.''

Layne's eyes were on Kyle, and she saw the fleeting pain that crossed his face at Robbie's words. This morning, Wheatlands had been his home. It wasn't going to be as easy to transplant the child as Kyle had hoped. Layne felt no triumph.

"And he won't come back," Robbie finished grimly. "Because he didn't like it here. He hated the kennel.''

She knelt beside him and wiped tears off his cheeks. "We'll find him, Rob. Let's go look.''

Kyle glanced at his watch. "You seem to have forgotten that I have a plane to catch, Layne.''

She stared at him. "So take your car. Or call a cab. Or hitchhike. I'm going to look for a dog. Come on, Rob.'' Neither of them looked back as they crossed the hall.

CHAPTER EIGHT

THEY looked for hours, driving the winding streets of Mission Hills, stopping to talk to people on the pavements. Every time Layne braked the car beside a dog-walking neighbour, Robbie's eyes filled with tears.

Layne could have cheerfully ripped Kyle to shreds with her fingernails. How could he have been so callous? A missing dog was no small thing to an eight-year-old child, especially a child as sensitive as Robbie. Beast had been his companion and confidante for three years, since the day he had come home from kindergarten with the dog at his heels and said, "He followed me home, Mom. Can I keep him?"

Until then Layne had always thought the line no more than a cartoon gag. But the little boy had looked at her with melting appeal in his earnest blue eyes, and the big dog had grinned at her, his tongue lolling and beady eyes almost hidden by his hair, and she had found herself saying yes. It was a decision she hadn't regretted, even in the days when grocery money was tight and Beast seemed to eat more than his share of it.

Robbie pushed the hair out of his eyes and said, "He was mean to Beast. That's why the dog ran away."

Layne caught herself and bit her lip. She'd been about to agree with Robbie, but what he had said wasn't strictly true. It was an ideal opportunity to foster discontent between father and son. It would serve Kyle right.

But she couldn't do it, Layne knew. The same force that had made her, all these years, be absolutely truthful to Robbie would not let her do this now. This was a way to take her revenge on Kyle for what he was doing to her—but Robbie would be the one to suffer most, if she helped destroy his faith in his father.

"Robbie, that isn't true. It isn't being mean to a dog to insist that he live outside—not a big dog like Beast. Your father might be wrong about him, but he wasn't cruel."

Robbie's eyes filled with tears again. Poor little guy, Layne thought. Right now he needs somebody to blame for it. Nevertheless, she was not going to let him blame Kyle.

They were driving through one of Kansas City's greenbelt parks, the long, narrow strips of parkland that brightened the city's streets. Off to the side, behind a sculpture, Layne saw a flash of movement and slowed the car.

Robbie saw it too. He sat up straight, peering out the window, then sat back with a sigh. "It isn't him, Mom."

Layne didn't question his judgment, but she did pull the little station wagon into the park and shut it off. "Robbie," she said gently, "we've driven miles and miles and searched for hours. We haven't seen Beast, but we might even have driven right by him."

"I would have seen him," Robbie insisted.

"I'm certain you think that, Rob. But the fact is, we could have missed him. We've hunted all over, but we just can't cover every placed." She rumpled his hair and tried to pull his tense little body into a hug, but he re-sisted. "I think we should go home and call the animal pound, so that they know we've lost Beast. Then all the city's dogcatchers will be looking for him."

"No!" Robbie cried. "I don't want him to be in the pound!"

"Robbie, there isn't any way to keep him out of there." Layne searched for a way to explain it to him.

"I bet he went home."

"Rob, I doubt very much he went back to Wheatlands. He must be enjoying his freedom too much to walk straight back into the kennel."

"I don't mean Wheatlands. I mean home. When you said we should go home, I thought that's what Beast would do."

"Oh. The old house?"

"Yes. He was happy there. Please, Mom?" His voice was a frantic plea.

Layne glanced at her watch. They'd already missed dinner, she thought, so what difference did it make if they spent another half hour driving back out to Clare's? If it would make Robbie happy, it was worth it. "All right, Robbie," she conceded. "But if he isn't there, then we go straight home—straight back to Wheatlands, I mean—and call the pound."

"All right," he agreed. "I just know he's there, Mom."

"You're giving the mutt credit for a terrific sense of direction," Layne murmured.

"Don't call him a mutt," Robbie requested politely. "Gary always called him that, and Beast didn't like it. Gary didn't like Beast either. But Clare did. She'll take care of him for me."

Layne didn't answer. She didn't want to point to Robbie just how many intersections and freeways and heavily trafficked streets there would have been for Beast to cross. He might never find his beloved dog.

But Robbie was convinced that he was right, and now

that he felt it was just a matter of minutes till he had Beast back, he was happy again. He chattered as they drove along, breaking into song once. Layne didn't have the heart to disillusion him. "This is a terrific car, isn't it, Mom?" he asked. "A lot better than The Tank."

"Much."

"It was nice of Dad to buy it for you, wasn't it? Maybe I can see Tony tonight."

"You could have seen Tony today when I came, if you hadn't been more interested in the treehouse. How is the treehouse coming along, anyway?"

"We didn't get finished. We just built the platform and a ladder so we can get up and down till the stairs are done. But Dad promised we'd finish it this weekend. It's going to be the world's best treehouse. Wait till it's finished! Can I sleep out there?"

"We'll see, when it's finished. And when the cast is off."

"Why does everything have to wait till the cast is off?"

"Because it prevents you from getting around as you should, and it isn't safe for you to be up a tree all night by yourself when you can't move as fast as usual."

"I can climb up and down the ladder just fine," Robbie pointed out reasonably.

"The answer is still no, Rob." Layne pulled the car into Clare's drive, behind Gary's. Oh, no, she thought. If there is one thing I don't need tonight, it's Gary. "Go scout around the neighbourhood, Robbie," she suggested. "I'll talk to Clare."

"So you can drink coffee," Robbie suggested cheekily.

"So I can see if Tony will come and help you," Layne finished, pretending not to notice the interruption.

Clare came around the house from the back yard. "Did you get my message?" she called.

"No—what message?"

"I found a little something of yours…"

"Beast!" Robbie screamed and took off for the back yard, crutches flying.

"Beast," Clare confirmed.

"How did he ever get here? I wouldn't have thought Beast had it in him."

Clare shrugged. "The homing instinct is a strong one. And Beast is no dummy. He picked out good old soft-hearted Robbie to follow home from school that day, didn't he?"

"Good point." They followed Robbie back to the patio, where Gary was sitting, feet up on the picnic table, a can of beer in his hand. "Well, hello, stranger," he said and made a half-hearted move to stand up.

"Don't bother," Layne told him, and picked out a chair for herself.

Gary settled back into his chair. "Have a beer?"

"No, thanks." Kyle, she thought, would have been on his feet before she had a chance to tell him not to stand for her; he had beautiful manners. But what good were the manners, she asked herself, when the man underneath didn't care a rap for common courtesy? Manners to Kyle were just that; they were certainly not the symbol of concern for his fellow human beings.

"I'm glad to see you haven't forgotten your way to the old neighbourhood," he said.

"Gary, don't waste your time on sarcasm. You know quite well why I'm not still living across the driveway, and I don't plan to explain it again."

"Good for you," Clare told her. "Gary's been crying

into that beer for a couple of hours now. I'm drinking sangria, Layne. Want a glass?''

"Of course." She followed Clare into the kitchen. "What's eating him?"

Clare took a pitcher from the refrigerator. "Oh, he had the rest of his life all planned out, and then you had to go throw a wrench into it." She handed Layne a brimming balloon glass, and smiled. "That's all."

"Is he drinking a lot?"

"No. At least he isn't while he's here. He's still on his first beer. Which is more than I can say for myself." She refilled her own glass with sangria. "Did you get the message I left at Wheatlands?"

"No. I've been out looking for the dog since I got home." Then, aching with curiosity, she added, "Who did you talk to?" Had Kyle cancelled his trip because of Robbie's dog?

"One of the maids."

"I wonder if Kyle was there, or if he went on to Minneapolis," Layne said thoughtfully.

"He was gone. I asked for him when the maid told me you weren't there. Did you just drive out here on a hunch?"

"Not exactly, Robbie was certain this was where Beast would have come. It made sense, but I wasn't as sure as he was that Beast could find his way."

"The dog didn't seem to be suffering any confusion. Look, I know you don't owe Gary any explanations, but perhaps you should give him a chance to talk to you. He has something on his mind that he won't tell me about."

"The perfect ending to a perfect day," Layne groaned. "But you're probably right."

He was still sitting on the terrace, still sipping the

beer, still maintaining his thoughtful silence. Layne sat down and looked out over the yard. The two boys were wrestling with the dog on the grass. For a moment, she closed her eyes and let the sounds and smells of summer carry her back to the old days. That last day of peace, before Robbie broke his ankle, when her biggest concern had been looking for a new job...

"Clare explained it to me," Gary said. "Is the game still over when Labor Day comes?"

Layne opened her eyes and nodded.

"What will you do then?"

She sipped her sangria and considered it. It was funny, actually, that she hadn't given much thought to what would happen to her after the first Monday in September. But of course there was nothing she could do about it now, while she and Kyle were still maintaining the pretence. She could hardly start applying for jobs. She was almost afraid to think about what she would do, for fear she would let it slip to Robbie, or to Stephen, that the way they were living was only an act.

"I suppose I'll get a job. Look for an apartment. Wait for my divorce." She shrugged. "Pick up the pieces of my life and put it back together—without Robbie."

Gary drained the beer can. "You didn't mention Kyle."

"Should I have? What about him?"

"Will it be difficult to put your life back together without him?"

"No." It was flat and uncompromising. "He hasn't been in my life for nine years. One summer isn't going to change that."

"You're living with him now."

"Under the same roof. It's hardly the same thing; Wheatlands has a pretty large roof."

"Do you really think he'll take Robbie?"

"He already has, Gary. He won't let me take him away." Her voice wasn't despairing or self-pitying, just factual. Kyle had told her what he planned to do, and he would do it.

"After you're free...will you want to see me?" The question was hesitant, almost fearful.

Layne looked to him over the brim of her glass, sipping her wine to give herself a chance to think. Gary wasn't Prince Charming, but he had been good to her—and good for her—in the last year. She had been almost a recluse, and Gary had forced her to get out of the house, to do things and to make new friends. If it hadn't been for Gary and Clare, she thought, her whole life would have been focused on Robbie. Losing Robbie would be a terrible blow to her, but she would survive it. A year ago it would have been even harder to bear.

"It doesn't matter, Layne. What you're doing this summer, I mean. I was terribly jealous, but I had no right to be. And no reason to be, either. If you tell me it's nothing but show, I believe that." He reached for her hand.

Layne let him hold it. "Of course I want to see you in the autumn, Gary, when this is over," she said. "We've been good friends, and..."

"Can we be more than friends? I still want to marry you, Layne."

Gary would never let her down. He would never hurt her, never set out to make her life miserable as Kyle seemed to delight in doing. Gary was a rock.

Robbie appeared at the edge of the patio. "Can Tony come home with us and stay overnight, Mom? He wants to see the treehouse." He saw Layne pull her hand away from Gary's, and he frowned.

"It's all right with me, if Clare approves." The boys disappeared into the house. Kyle probably won't like the idea, she thought, but then who cares? He didn't tell me not to allow Robbie's friends to stay at Wheatlands. Interesting, she thought, that Robbie is already calling Wheatlands home again.

Had the child's glance at Gary been merely unfriendly, or was he now actively hostile? Probably hostile, Layne decided. Robbie would disapprove of anything that came between his parents right now, and Gary was a primary target. If she decided to marry Gary, Robbie would just have to get used to it...

But it really wouldn't be any of Robbie's business, she realised. If Robbie wasn't living with her, then she didn't have to consider how he felt about it.

"I don't know, Gary. I can't make any plans to start a new marriage until this one is over and done with."

He smiled. "I know, honey. It's all right. You're uncomfortable talking about it, and frankly, so am I. So we'll just call it a quiet understanding, and we won't talk about it till you're free." He patted her hand.

That wasn't what I meant at all, Layne wanted to say, but before she found the words Clare came out with a pitcher of sangria and refilled her glass. "Did you give permission for an overnight stay?"

"Sure. Tony can come home with us if he likes."

"All right. I just wanted to make sure they weren't running the old what's-for-supper con."

"What's that?" Gary asked.

"The boys came up with that one when they were four. They would ask each of us what was on the menu, and coincidentally on the nights that we were having something Tony didn't like, he was always invited over to Robbie's house to eat. And vice versa. It took us weeks to catch on.''

"If they hadn't so consistently avoided liver, we probably never would have,'' Layne mused.

"Kids,'' Gary grunted. "Can I have another beer, Clare?''

"Certainly, if you go after it yourself.'' Clare sat down with a sigh and put her feet up. "Did you have a good talk?'' she asked when Gary had gone inside.

Layne shrugged. "Gary hears only what he wants to.''

"We're ready, Mom,'' Robbie said as he burst out the door. "And I'm hungry! We never had supper.''

"I wondered how long it would take you to notice. Go put Beast in the back of the car.'' Layne handed him the keys. "I'll be there in a minute.''

"I'll pick Tony up tomorrow,'' Clare said.

Layne gave her a quick hug. "Come for lunch, then, so we can talk. I'd better take this crowd to the Burger Barn before they eat the upholstery.''

The boys and Beast consumed sandwiches and fries at a rate that appalled Layne. When she pulled Mr Hamburg's ten-dollar bill out of her wallet, she was beginning to regret having thrown Kyle's money back at him. He'd had no right to cut off her only source of income, but it was done. There would be no more spending money from Mr Hamburg, and pride or no pride, she was about three days away from being broke. She'd be forced to apologise to Kyle and ask for an allowance.

Well, she told herself finally, he wouldn't be back for a few days. She'd handle that when she got to it.

Tony was properly impressed by the floodlighted exterior of Wheatlands, and Robbie promptly took him on a tour. They were in such a rush that they nearly bowled over the little uniformed maid who came hurrying down the hall to the front entrance.

"Robert!" Layne ordered. "Where are your manners?"

He turned around. "Sorry," he said and was gone down the hall.

The maid didn't seem to notice. "Oh, Mrs Emerson," she breathed. "Mr Kyle has been calling and calling…he was terribly upset that you weren't home yet. And Mr Stephen has been concerned too."

That Stephen had been frightened tore at Layne's heart. He had enough problems; why hadn't she been thoughtful enough to call? She looked at the big grandfather clock. It was after eleven; plenty late for Stephen to be up. And as for Kyle checking up on her—

She dashed up the stairs and tapped at Stephen's door. The young male nurse answered it. The relief on his face was apparent.

Did everyone think we'd been kidnapped, Layne wondered. "David, just tell Mr Stephen we're home safe, dog and all, and that I'll be in to see him tomorrow," she said.

"He's been very worried, Mrs Emerson. We all have."

"I'm sorry to have upset everyone. Robbie and I have lived alone for so long, we didn't think anyone would pay any attention if we were late."

"Around here," David said gently, "everyone pays attention."

"I'd forgotten," Layne mused. "What did the doctor say?"

David shrugged. "He changed the pain medication. But sometimes nothing that doctors can do seems to make any difference at all. That's one of the frustrating things about rheumatoid arthritis, Mrs Emerson. It can come and go suddenly, with no reason whatever.''

''It must be so difficult for him. And yet he doesn't complain.''

''He gets depressed sometimes. Not as much now that you and Robbie are here, though. I'll tell him that you'll see him in the morning.''

It was time to get the boys into bed, she realised as she approached Robbie's room. Muffled conversation was coming from behind the door, and it died instantly as she tapped. ''Robbie? May I come in?''

The boys were already in their pyjamas, which utterly astonished her. Robbie had graciously given up the top bunk to his guest, and Tony was sitting on the edge of it, swinging his feet. Robbie was already sprawled across the lower bunk, and he scarcely opened his eyes as he murmured, ''Gosh, I'm tired, Mom. See you in the morning.''

''What's going on, Rob?'' Layne was suspicious.

Robbie's big blue eyes opened wide. ''What do you mean?''

''I mean, you're up to something, Robert Baxter Emerson.'' Then she relented. ''But if it gets you to bed without protest, I guess I'll worry about it in the morning.'' She leaned over to kiss him goodnight, and something wet and rough scraped across her ankle. Layne jerked upright and hit her head on the top bunk.

''Did you hurt yourself, Layne?'' Tony asked anxiously.

''No, but I'm probably going to hurt whatever it was that licked me.'' She pulled Robbie's sheet back and peered under the bed. Beast's beady black eyes laughed back at her. There was scarcely room for the big dog.

She draped the sheet over Robbie and said, ''I didn't

see a thing, Robert. But you be sure he's in the kennel when your father gets home the day after tomorrow. Then you may discuss with him whether Beast stays in the house. And leave me out of it.''

"Yes, Mom." And as she closed the door behind her, she heard a sleepy, "Thanks, Mom."

The phone was ringing beside Kyle's bed. She carried it over to the dressing table and let it ring seven times before she decided that the staff had all gone on vacation. She might as well answer it, she decided. If there was one thing Kyle was, it was persistent; he'd call till three in the morning if she wanted to push him that far.

"So you finally got home," he said as soon as she picked it up.

"I didn't realise I had a curfew." Layne reached for her cold cream and started patting it on her face.

"Where have you been?"

"Looking for the dog."

"I presume you found him or you'd still be looking. What is so darned valuable about that mutt?"

"I'd advise you not to call him a mutt when Robbie can hear you. He has a prejudice against people who don't understand Beast's worth."

Kyle grunted. "I suppose that means the dog is sleeping on the foot of his bed right now."

"He most certainly isn't." Layne was proud of the note of artistic distaste in her voice. "Robbie knows quite well how you feel about Beast being in the house." And besides, she told herself, Beast isn't on the bed, he's under it.

"Why don't I believe you?"

"When you figure it out, let me know. How was your flight?"

"Like most of them. When they invent a faster way

of getting from one city to another, I'm going to invest in it.'' He hesitated, as if wondering if she'd be interested, then added, ''I've already got a look at the site, by the way. It's near the airport, so we drove by.''

''Does it look promising?''

''Yes. It's a good location for a shopping centre. But I don't know if I want to build it. It's a long way from home.''

''A long way from Robbie, you mean?''

There was a brief pause. ''Yeah. A long way from Robbie.'' He sounded a little gruff.

He really does love Robbie, she realised. ''He misses you already, Kyle. He was angry when you left, but he's over it now.'' Amazing, she thought, that it was so much easier to talk to him on the phone.

''Well, I miss him too. Tell him I'll see him tomorrow.''

''Tomorrow? So soon? I thought you were coming home on Thursday.''

He sounded half-amused, half-angry. ''I am, Layne. But it's after midnight—so it's actually Wednesday right now.''

''Oh. Sorry.''

''No, you're not sorry. You're relieved. But at least you're honest, Layne.'' He hesitated. ''I am glad that you found the dog. Sleep well.''

''You too, Kyle. See you tomorrow.''

She put the phone down slowly, a little puzzled by his attitude. Then she realised that perhaps it was easier for Kyle, too, when they weren't in the same room. At least she couldn't throw money at him over the telephone.

I might even miss him, she thought as she went to make her bed on the long couch in the sitting room.

Then she shook her head ruefully. How could she miss the constant conflict and the need to be always on guard when he was there?

She pulled sheets and a light blanket out of the small chest that served as a coffee table, and then stopped short. Kyle was in Minneapolis. Why should she spend another night in discomfort on that couch when he would never know—or care—where she slept?

She was tucked into the big canopied bed and half-asleep when suddenly it came to her. The tone of Kyle's voice had been almost forlorn. He had sounded lonely.

"Oh, don't be ridiculous, Layne," she told herself crossly. "He's no more lonely than you are—unless he's missing Jessica."

She punched the pillow into her favourite shape and dropped off into her first sound sleep in three weeks.

CHAPTER NINE

STEPHEN was on the sun porch, the breeze coming in through wide windows and ruffling his white hair. He looked up with a smile as Layne came in. "You had us frightened last night, young woman," he scolded, but his tone was light.

"I'm sorry. I didn't even think about calling, because I didn't realise anyone would notice."

"You do have a history of disappearing abruptly, Layne," he said gently.

"Oh." She pulled up a small chair and sat down beside him. "Do you know, I'd forgotten all about that."

"The rest of us haven't."

Layne was afraid that he would pursue it further, but Stephen Emerson was too sensitive a man to push her for an explanation she certainly didn't want to give.

"I'm glad Robbie found his dog. Beast is obviously very fond of him." He pointed through the window. Beast dropped the stick in Robbie's lap, then nudged the boy down on his back and started to lick his face. Layne could almost hear Robbie's shrieks of delight as the rough tongue tickled his face. It was one of their favourite games.

"I wish Kyle could understand how important the dog is," she mused. "Robbie was so angry yesterday he wanted to move back to our old house."

Stephen said thoughtfully, "Perhaps I should remind Kyle of Killer."

"Who on earth is Killer?"

"He was Kyle's dog. The neighbour's dog, actually. He was a German shepherd, and they'd bought him to protect their property. Killer would have done his best, too—he'd have licked a burglar to death. But he kept running away. He'd get out of his pen somehow and come straight here. Eventually they just gave him to Kyle." He looked thoughtful. "Yes, perhaps I should remind him. He probably hasn't thought about Killer in ten years."

"I'm sure Robbie would be grateful. Beast isn't exactly appropriate for Wheatlands, but he is Robbie's best friend. I don't think Kyle understands that."

Stephen shifted in his chair, and Layne saw a flicker of pain cross his face. "I'll see what I can do. Robbie brought his young friend in to see me this morning. A nice child, but a quiet one. He hardly said a word. Or was he just shy?"

"No, Tony has always been quiet. They're almost opposites, aren't they? Robbie misses him so—I wish Tony could have stayed a week, but Clare took him home a few minutes ago."

"Robbie will soon find friends here."

"Oh, he already has." She wondered if Kyle would forbid Robbie to see his old friends. Once she was gone, he would want no reminders of what Robbie's life had been. Perhaps that was what really lay behind his dislike of Beast, too.

Stephen was looking out across the wide lawn where Robbie and Beast were playing. "How are the plans for the garden party coming along?"

All right. But I was obviously never cut out to be a

society hostess. I'm uncomfortable with things like this.''

"Only because you aren't used to them. The more parties you give, the more you will enjoy them, and the easier they'll be.''

Layne's voice was doubting. "If you say so." But she was thinking. Thank God this is the only party I'll be responsible for. When I'm on my own again, I can go back to hamburgers on the grill and friends dropping in.

"Layne, you have everything you need, except confidence. Once that comes, you'll be unbeatable. Garden parties aren't so bad.''

"Prove it," she challenged. "Come down and help entertain all these people. Otherwise, I refuse to believe that you think they're anything but a waste of time.''

Stephen laughed. "All right. I'll come down for your party, if I feel up to it. No promises yet, though. I'm waiting to see if this new medication does the trick.''

"Is there much pain?''

"It isn't bad today. Part of it is worry, I think. I start fretting about my condition, and that makes it hurt worse. I'd enjoy your party. It's been years since Kyle has entertained here.''

She looked at him in surprise. What do you mean?

"On this scale," he added smoothly. "Everyone in Kansas City who has an ounce of influence or political power or pedigree will be coming to that garden party. If anyone misses, you can bet he didn't get the invitation.''

"If you're trying to reassure me, Stephen, you're failing. I'm getting more nervous by the minute.''

"They're coming to your house, Layne. At your command.''

"At Kyle's command.''

"And then the dinner afterwards..."

Layne sighed. "Which I would give anything to avoid," she said. "But Kyle insisted. Who am I to entertain the governor? He'll probably be yawning into his soup."

"There's the lack of confidence again," Stephen scolded. "Governor Howard has always had an eye for a pretty lady; he would probably be delighted to sit and look at you if all you did was smile at him."

Layne folded her arms. "Has anyone told you that you're a bit prejudiced, Stephen?"

"I am not in the least prejudiced. I am, however, observant. You might watch out for Jessica Tate that night, Layne. She is also observant, and she has grown to think of Cam Howard as her personal property."

"I watch out for Jessica every minute of every day."

"Do you still think that she's after Kyle?"

No, Layne thought. I know she is. And Kyle isn't much opposed to the idea, once he can get rid of me.

But she didn't argue. Perhaps if she agreed with Stephen, he'd stop trying to convince her.

"By the way, Layne, would you do something for me?"

"Of course."

He called to the nurse in the next room. "Dave, bring me my wallet, please." He turned to Layne. "Robbie tells me that there is a marvellous baseball glove down at the sports shop. I want him to have it."

"Stephen, I don't like for him to ask you for things. It's bad manners, and he knows better."

"He didn't ask. We were talking about his baseball career, and he merely told me about the glove. I'm the one who thinks he should have it." David brought the wallet, and Stephen extracted a bill and pressed it into Layne's hand.

"You spoil him," she said, twisting the bill.

"I'm an old man, Layne, and a sick one. Sometimes in the last couple of years it has seemed to me that just living another day was too difficult. But now that I've got a chance to know Robbie, I won't give up. It's too much fun to see him grow and learn and change." He stared out the window and added softly, "I have eight years to make up, Layne. Please let me spoil him a little."

She looked down at the bill crumpled in her palm. Her throat was too choked to speak. She knew that Stephen wondered why she had left Kyle years ago. But never had he asked, never had he so much as hinted to her that he resented missing out on his grandson's early years. "Of course, Stephen," she whispered. "Whatever you want." Then she looked closely at the bill in her hand. "You gave me a hundred dollars."

"I know," Stephen agreed. "It's supposed to be quite a glove."

Layne tucked it into the pocket of her shorts. "I'll get the change back to you as soon as I can. I don't know if I can take him today, but..."

"The rest of the money is for you, Layne. I'd like to spoil you a little, too, but you don't talk to me about baseball gloves, or whatever it is that you dream of." His smile was affectionate. "So you'll have to decide what kind of spoiling you need."

She kissed his forehead. "Thank you." She was almost too choked up to say it.

"But it isn't allowed to be anything you would buy for yourself," he warned. "That money is strictly for extras. Understood?"

Layne nodded. What Stephen didn't know right now, she thought, was that everything looked like a luxury to her right now. Suddenly her heart was singing. It meant that she didn't have to go back to Kyle, hat in hand, and apologise. Stephen's gift, if she used it carefully, would take her through the next few weeks.

"I took the liberty of setting up a trust for him, by the way, Layne, just to be certain that his education is provided for. I wanted to be sure that Robbie has the resources to be whatever he wants to be."

Was Stephen concerned that Kyle would try to force Robbie into the construction business? Whatever his reasons, Layne had to admit relief. It would give Robbie some independence from his father, if that was what he wanted.

Stephen saw the thoughtful look on her face and added. "The trust is written to include other children, too, if you and Kyle have others. It would hardly be fair of me to assume that Robbie will be the only one."

Before she could answer, Robbie tapped on the half-open door of the sun porch and came in. "I'm bored, Mom," he announced. Beast was beside him, his tongue hanging out after their game.

Layne ran her fingers through the child's hair. "Only boring people get bored, Robbie. There are a hundred things to do. Shall we make a list?"

"I know what I want to do. I want to bake cookies with you. But when I was in the kitchen, Mrs Andrews told me to leave."

"Well, I don't see why we shouldn't be able to bake cookies. Do you?" she asked Stephen.

"Can't think of a single reason. Mrs Andrews makes good cookies, too, however."

Robbie shook his head. "No, Grandpa, you don't see.

Mrs Andrews skimps on the nuts and stuff, Mom never does. And besides, Mom, and I always talk when we bake cookies, and that makes them extra good. It always tastes better when you do it yourself, doesn't it, Mom?''

''It seems to work that way. What kind will it be today?''

''Chocolate chip,'' Robbie decided. ''And then…''

''Hold it right there,'' Layne warned. ''Chocolate chip it is, and only that.''

Robbie grinned. ''It was worth a try,'' he shrugged. ''Can Beast help?''

''Beast may lie in a corner and watch and clean up the one or two cookies that might get dropped. Fair enough?''

''Sure. We'll bring you a cookie, Grandpa.''

''You'd better. I'll be interested in testing your recipe.''

Mrs Andrews looked up forbiddingly as the two of them came into the kitchen, Beast trailing along behind. ''Yes, Ma'am?'' she said frostily.

Layne was determined to be tactful, but firm. ''We're going to bake cookies, Mrs Andrews. Where can we work so that we won't be in your way?''

The cook shook her head. ''I'm quite sorry, Mrs Emerson, but I haven't time for such nonsense today. And I'd appreciate it, young man, if you took that dog out of my kitchen.''

Robbie didn't seem to hear her. Layne counted to ten. ''I'm not asking you to bake the cookies or clean up the mess, Mrs Andrews,'' she said quietly. ''We will do all the work. All we need is a corner of the kitchen so we can do it.''

''And I said there isn't one. You'd be in my way.'' The cook calmly went back to her task. She was cutting up vegetables for a salad. The knife she was using looked like a lethal weapon. There was no other evidence that dinner preparation was under way.

Layne looked around at the big kitchen. The stainless steel was polished to a gleam, and the butcher block counters were spotless. Copper-bottomed pans hung from racks above the working areas. There were two of everything, even a spare dishwasher for the big parties. If pushed, Mrs Andrews could cook for the Third Army there. There was certainly room for them to bake cookies. And Layne was not about to back down this time.

"Robbie, wash your hands," she ordered, and started to look through drawers for an apron to tie around him.

"Mrs Emerson," the cook said, and put down the knife. She was no longer so calm. "Please stop rummaging through my kitchen."

"Your kitchen?" Layne asked. Her voice was deceptively calm, and she didn't stop opening drawers.

"Well, it certainly isn't yours!"

"How did you come to that conclusion?"

"Just who do you think you are, anyway, coming in here and telling everybody what to do?" Mrs Andrews was turning red with anger. "You're certainly not the mistress of this house—you're nothing at all! Who do you think you're fooling? You don't even sleep in Mr Kyle's bed except when he's gone."

Layne found the apron and tied it carefully around Robbie, feeling the tension in his muscles. He might not understand what Mrs Andrews meant—she certainly hoped he didn't—but he knew it was venomous.

Layne patted his shoulder reassuringly and stood up. "Mrs Andrews, you're fired. You can pick up your cheque at the employment office tomorrow. Don't bother to stay for dinner; I'll take care of it."

The woman's mouth dropped open. It was plain that she had not expected this. "Mr Kyle...he won't like this," she stammered. "He won't stand for it. You've got no authority to fire me."

"We'll just have to wait and see what he says. If Mr Emerson wishes to rehire you, that will of course be his option. He'll be home tomorrow if you care to call him." She turned to Robbie. "Chocolate chip, I believe you said?"

He grinned and waited till Mrs Andrews had departed before saying, "A virtuosos performance, Mom!"

"And just where did you get that word?" Layne was rummaging in the refrigerator. Veal cutlets, she was thinking. The menu had said they were having veal... Here they are. Well, she certainly could handle that.

"From Grandpa. He says my vocabulary is lousy."

"I somehow doubt that he phrased it that way. We're going to have to get to work, Robbie, if we're going to get cookies baked. We now have dinner to cook, too."

"Now I can run!" Robbie carolled as he and Layne came out of Dr Morgan's office on to the sun-baked street. "And without those awful crutches, I can do almost anything!"

"You are still wearing a cast, however," Layne warned, "and it still hasn't hardened completely." She wondered if she was sounding like a cracked record. She certainly felt like one.

"Yeah, but it's a walking cast," Robbie said.

"And why do you suppose it isn't called a running cast?" Layne asked. "Because you aren't supposed to be running, that's why. Another three weeks of good behaviour and you can do whatever you like."

"But by that time the summer will be over." Robbie's face was long.

"No, it won't. And I know how difficult it has been to go through a summer without running or baseball or swimming. It will certainly be one to remember, won't it?"

The little face brightened. "Dad said he was going to enclose the pool this autumn, so it'll be heated. We can swim all winter."

"I wouldn't plan on it." Why waste her breath, Layne thought.

"Are we going to the airport now?" Robbie did a sudden little hop.

"No skipping allowed, Rob." She unlocked the car door. "No, we're going back to Wheatlands first because your dad's plane isn't due in for a couple of hours. And I need to get dinner underway."

"Didn't you hire that woman this morning?"

"No. I asked her if she could make baked Alaska and she said she'd never been there. I didn't think she was suitable for the job."

"Oh." Robbie thought that over. "Why did she have to go to Alaska to be a cook?"

"Forget it, Rob."

"Okay." He whistled and watched Kansas City go by for a few minutes, then broke off abruptly. "I forgot— Grandpa said to tell you that since you came upstairs for dinner with us last night we'd dress up and come down for dinner with you and Dad tonight."

"That's very thoughtful of him." It was enough trouble for the staff to prepare two dinners every night; for her to do it by herself—especially today, with the new cast and Kyle to pick up at the airport—would have been impossible. Bless Stephen for thinking of it.

"But what if I don't want to dress up?"

"Unless you take a bath and put on a clean shirt and probably a tie, you will have dinner in the kitchen while I'm putting the finishing touches on it."

She had hoped to have a cook hired in time to prepare tonight's meal, but the two applicants the employment office had sent this morning had been impossible. So she was just going to have to do it herself and hope that Kyle didn't get angry. If she was lucky, he might not even notice. And if she could once get a cook hired and installed in the kitchen, she didn't think he would care an iota whether it was Mrs Andrews or not. The thing that was guaranteed to make him angry was if there was no one in the kitchen.

Well, there was another applicant coming this afternoon. Perhaps she would be lucky.

"Can Beast come to the airport to meet Dad?" Robbie asked as he caught sight of the big dog waiting mournfully in the kennel.

"I don't think that would be wise. You'd better leave him in the kennel again."

"But he hates the kennel. And I hate to put him in it."

"Would you rather have him run away again?"

"No. Do you think Dad will change his mind about Beast?"

"I stopped predicting what your father would do a long time ago, Robbie." She shut the car off and picked up her handbag. "Don't forget your new baseball glove. And be sure to stop up and show it to Grandpa right away."

"And remember to say thank you," Robbie added, before she had a chance. "Now that I don't need the crutches, I can start practising again. Maybe Dad will pitch for me when he gets home.''

She went straight to the kitchen, the long list of things yet to be done running through her mind. She'd never get finished, she thought despairingly. The wait at the doctor's office had thrown her off schedule.

The little maid caught her at the kitchen door. ''The lady's here about the cook's job.''

Layne glanced at her watch. ''All right. Send her in; I'll have to work while I talk to her.''

''She's already in the kitchen,'' the maid said.

A cheerful voice greeted her from the butcher block island in the centre of the kitchen. A grey-haired woman was sitting on a high stool there, inserting whole cloves into the top of a Virginia ham. ''I hope you'll pardon me, Mrs Emerson,'' she said. ''I saw your list lying here, and it looked to me as if an extra pair of hands might be welcome. So I brewed myself some tea and started in.''

Layne was taken aback. ''Mrs Kirk?''

''Carolyn Kirk. My references are on the table, over there.''

Layne flipped through them. It didn't surprise her that they were impressive; Mrs Kirk was impressive all by herself.

''There's tea in the pot, if you'd like some. Now, what sort of cook are you looking for?''

''How many kinds are there?'' Layne asked weakly.

Carolyn Kirk smiled. ''Dozens, I suppose, I should have phrased it a little differently. What sort of cooking do you need done? This kind of thing?'' She gestured towards the ham.

''Mostly it's just family meals, but there will be occasional dinner parties. We're having one next week for the governor—there will be eighteen for dinner, and I'd planned on Chicken Wellington.''

''A good choice. You could serve Chicken Wellington to eight hundred and do a good job. Anything elaborate for dessert?''

''The governor's favourite is baked Alaska.''

Robbie and Beast came in just then. ''Have you been to Alaska?'' he asked Mrs Kirk. ''I sure hope so, because then my mom can hire you and she won't have to cook dinner.''

Mrs Kirk scratched Beast's ears thoroughly. The dog looked disappointed when she got up to wash her hands. ''No, I haven't been there, but I can make a mean baked Alaska,'' she told Robbie. ''Just wait till you try it.''

Robbie was unconvinced. ''Do you bake cookies? And fudge layer cakes?''

''I certainly do. And I make chocolate eclairs and cream puffs and Napoleons and cherries jubilee and...''

''Can I have them all?''

''Not all at once, no.''

Layne laughed. ''I think you just answered my other question. I'm looking for someone who will make my son feel at home in the kitchen, but who will exercise some prudence about what he eats here.'' In another few weeks, she reminded herself, she would no longer be there to keep an eye on him. Having someone like Mrs Kirk around would help.

''I raised four boys of my own,'' Mrs Kirk said dryly. ''Tell you what, Mrs Emerson. Why don't you turn tonight's dinner over to me, and after it's over we'll talk about the job.''

''I think that's a marvellous idea. I'll pay you for tonight, of course, whether you come to work for us or not.''

The woman shook her head. "If dinner isn't good enough to convince you, then you don't need to pay me."

"I'm on my way to the airport to meet my husband. He's the one you'll need to convince."

Mrs Kirk looked thoughtful. "Perhaps I'll whip up some hot rolls," she decided. "There's time for my special recipe."

"Good idea. Coming, Robbie?"

The airport was busy and planes were stacked, circling and waiting to land, but finally Kyle's flight was called. Layne glanced at her watch and was doubly thankful for Mrs Kirk.

"There he is," Robbie exclaimed and ran to meet his father. Layne studied Kyle's face, watching as the tiredness vanished to be replaced by vibrant joy as he saw his son.

Her heart twisted. Did she look like that when she first caught sight of Robbie, she wondered. She was glad for them, she told herself fiercely. It would make it easier for the child.

It was crazy to be jealous of Kyle when Robbie ran to him, she thought. Of course he was delighted to see his father. He was still playing a new game.

And then she thought, as she walked slowly towards them, that it was even crazier to be jealous of Robbie when Kyle swung the boy up into his arms with that passionate joy in his eyes. After all, she didn't expect Kyle to be thrilled at the sight of her.

And why, Layne Emerson, she scolded herself, should that make you feel so damn sad?

Kyle came towards her with a smile, Robbie still in his arms as if he couldn't bear to put him down. Layne's heart ached at the sight of them together, so very much alike.

Kyle set his briefcase down and let Robbie slide slowly to the floor. "Hi, Layne," he said and put his arms around her. "Aren't you going to welcome a tired traveller?"

Layne's eyes were wide with shock.

Kyle laughed. "I assure you, my lovely wife, that I do not intend to rape you here in the terminal," he murmured. His hands travelled gently across the small of her back, pressing her tight against him.

Every sensitive nerve ending screamed under his gentle touch. Why was he doing this, Layne wondered. What was he trying to prove? But she had no time to speculate on Kyle's reasons before he kissed her.

It was a lover's kiss, long and gentle, the one he had always used to tell her how desirable she was. He hasn't forgotten how, she thought, dazed by the assault. She was clinging to him to keep from falling, and he knew it. He smiled as he released her, shifting his hold until he was half-supporting her with one arm lightly around her waist.

"Have you had a pleasant, peaceful couple of days?" he asked. There was a cynical twist to his words, and she flinched at the sudden change in his attitude.

It's just a reminder that you're only here to meet him because he wanted Robbie, Layne told herself. Remember it, and act accordingly. But if he felt that way—why the kiss?

It was explained for her, however, before they left the terminal, when Kyle waved at a couple of associates and stopped to talk briefly to another. Layne was furious at having allowed herself to be used; Kyle had only been impressing his acquaintances with his image as a family man.

"Let's stop at North Winds," he suggested as they walked out to the car. "I think a small celebration is in order since we got rid of the crutches."

"Got another cast, though," Robbie said. He was proudly carrying Kyle's briefcase.

"Dr Morgan seems to have lost his mind," Layne added. She was still a little shaky, and staying on a neutral subject was safest. "Robbie promised to be very careful of the cast, and Dr Morgan believed that he meant it."

"Is the ankle healing?"

"Yes, but he wants the walking cast on for three more weeks."

"My summer will be all gone," Robbie mourned.

Kyle put Robbie into the back of the little station wagon and stretched out in the passenger seat.

"Why should I? You're perfectly capable. How's the Beast, Robbie? Has he recovered from his adventure?"

"He's okay." Robbie's tone was wary. He caught Layne's eyes in the driving mirror; he looked scared. "Dad…"

"I suppose he's been sleeping on your bed?"

"Well…" Robbie searched for a way out, then blurted, "No, sir. He's been under it, Mom didn't know."

Layne could feel Kyle watching her, and she fought against letting herself go red with embarrassment.

"Of course your mother knew, Robbie," he said finally. "Mothers always know."

Now we're both in the soup, Layne thought. I wonder what the price will be.

"Are we still going to North Winds?" she asked as

they approached the freeway exit that led to the shopping centre.

He looked surprised that she had asked. "Of course. If we expect Beast to stay off the human-type furniture, then we'll have to buy him a bed of his own, won't we?"

"Daddy!" Robbie screamed his happiness and tried to fling his arms around Kyle's neck.

"Robbie, for heaven's sake," Layne protested. "What made you change your mind, Kyle?"

"Oh, I had a dog once, too, as my father reminded me over the phone this morning. Killer was a lot of company for me."

"Stephen told me the dog would get out of his pen and come over to play with you."

"They never did find out how he escaped." She must have looked suspicious, and he laughed. "All right, I admit it. I taught him to climb the fence. He was a slow learner, but once he knew that trick there wasn't a pen in Mission Hills that could hold him."

Layne parked the car. "It won't take all three of us to choose a dog bed, will it?"

"Why? Want to look for something else?"

"Yes. I'll meet you in the main lobby, by the goldfish pool."

"Make it Felicity's and I'll buy you a drink."

"They won't let me into Felicity's dressed like this." Layne looked down at her printed shirt and faded jeans. She hadn't dressed up to meet Kyle; what was the use? He'd have laughed at her effort to impress him.

"Yes, they will. Just tell them you're with me."

She could go into Felicity's in a wet bikini if she was with Kyle, Layne fumed as she walked on down the mall.

The money Stephen had given her was burning a hole in her pocket. Despite what she had said about not wanting or needing new clothes, her pride was beginning to smart. She didn't want to show up at the governor's garden party in her old blue sundress. It might embarrass Kyle, but it would also embarrass her, and Layne was beginning to hate looking dowdy next to Jessica. And after all, as Kyle had said, even inexpensive clothes came in flattering colours.

Half an hour later, though, she was tired, frustrated and ready to cry. She'd been through two whole department stores, and there was nothing in either one of them which was inexpensive, flattering and the right size.

The money that had looked like a fortune an hour before lay heavily in her pocket as she walked past three boutiques on her way to Felicity's. She knew better than to even look in. If she saw something she liked, it would be far above her price range. Besides, one of those boutiques was Jessica's. And the way Layne's luck was running, she'd choose it for sure.

The old blue sundress would have to do. There was no other choice. She would not ask Kyle for the money to replace it.

Robbie was sipping a Shirley Temple and chattering to an indulgent Kyle, who was leaning back in his chair and lazily stirring a Scotch and water. He looked up as Layne approached the table and got to his feet to hold her chair.

"A Tom Collins for the lady," he told the waiter.

"You should see what we got, Mom," Robbie said. "Beast will love his new bed. It's blue velvet and everything."

"Surely not velvet?" Layne looked questioningly up at Kyle.

He nodded. "Only pampered pets shop at North Winds."

"He'd be just as happy with a blanket on the floor, Kyle. And I didn't know they made dog beds big enough for a sheepdog."

Kyle snapped his fingers. "Is *that* what Beast is? All this time I'd been thinking he was just a mutt."

"Layne smiled reluctantly. "Well, he's at least half sheepdog."

"In any case, he needn't apply for membership in the American Kennel Club. And by the way, I tried to talk Robbie out of the purchase he made for you."

"Oh?" Layne's voice was cool.

"Not because I didn't want you to have it. But it's about eight sizes too large, and I didn't want you to be mad at me." He looked her over closely, and Layne was thankful that her drink arrived just then. By the time she had taken her first sip, Kyle seemed to be finished with his assessment.

"I'd say you're still about a size five," he concluded. "Robbie's purchase is probably an eighteen."

"You'll love it, Mom." Robbie rummaged under the table and came up with a bag emblazoned with the name of the pet store.

Layne tore it open and pulled out a bright yellow T-shirt with a picture of a sleepy Persian kitten on a velvet cushion. The cat was thinking, "I am an Aristo-Cat."

"Thanks, Robbie," she said. "It'll make a perfect nightshirt."

"See?" Robbie told his father. "I knew it was the right size." He ate the fruit out of his Shirley Temple and said, "When am I going to get my computer?"

"Robert!" Layne said.

Kyle was undisturbed. "As soon as you can convince me that you need one."

Robbie thought it over for a moment. "How can I convince you?" he asked reasonably. "You won't even come and see what they can do."

Kyle looked at Layne with a raised eyebrow. "Go on," Layne said. "I'll be along when I've finished my drink."

"If you're sure you don't mind…" But they were gone before she could reply.

Even inexpensive clothes come in flattering colours. Layne stared into her glass and thought about it. Perhaps it was just the new mall that was so expensive, she thought. She still had several days before the party. Perhaps she could still find something.

"Mind if I sit down for a minute?" Jessica Tate didn't pause for an answer before taking the chair opposite Layne. She lit a cigarette, flicking the gold lighter carefully so she didn't damage her perfectly manicured nails. "Shopping for clothes, Layne? That's a perfectly…interesting…garment you were showing Kyle a moment ago."

Layne didn't answer.

"Perhaps you'd like me to take you to my boutique. I'm sure we could come up with the appropriate clothes for you." Even for you, the undertone said. The hard blue eyes focused on Layne's man-tailored shirt.

"Thank you, Jessica, but I believe I can shop for myself." It was an effort to keep her voice steady.

"Whatever you like." Jessica shrugged and stood up. Her little red dress, trimmed in white, was simple and well cut and perfect for an afternoon of casual shopping. It had probably cost more than Layne's whole wardrobe.

"Tell Kyle I'll drop in for an after-dinner drink tonight, to welcome him home."

What is the use? she thought when Jessica had gone. She stared into the bottom of her glass and fought to keep the tears out of her eyes. No matter what she wore, it could never compare to what Jessica had. The blue dress would be plenty good enough. At least then no one—especially not Kyle—would think she was trying to compete with Jessica.

CHAPTER TEN

I WISH Stephen and Robbie would come down to dinner more often, Layne found herself thinking by the time dessert was served. The mood at the table had been almost rollicking, instead of the silence she and Kyle usually shared.

Stephen winked at her as the maid put a generous serving of baked Alaska in front of him. "Is this a trial run for Cam Howard's party?" he asked. "My compliments to the lady in the kitchen."

"I'll tell her," Layne murmured. As far as she was concerned Mrs Kirk had a job. The meringue atop the dessert melted in her mouth.

"When are we going to another Royals game, Dad?" Robbie asked.

"Next week when they get back from the West Coast. Is that soon enough?"

"Okay," Robbie said with a flourish of his spoon. "And can I have my birthday party at the zoo?"

If Robbie expressed the desire, Layne thought, Kyle would probably buy the zoo for his birthday. The light in his eyes tonight as he watched his son twisted her heart.

"October will be a little late for a zoo party," Kyle said. "We'll see, Robbie."

"Mom will figure it out. She makes the best birthday parties," Robbie told him. "Last year we filled the whole house with balloons. I helped blow 'em up. Can I have balloons this year, too, Mom?''

Their eyes met across the length of the table, Layne's big and brown and pleading, Kyle's dark blue and cynical.

Then he frowned as he noticed the orange dress she was wearing. Layne lifted her shoulders in a tiny shrug; she had warned him, after all, that he would probably get tired of seeing Clare's dress. Though they didn't dress formally every night, it was still the only thing she owned which was suitable to grace the dinner table at Wheatlands, and he had certainly seen it often. Well, she decided, if it bothered him, that was his problem.

"We'll see about the balloons when your birthday comes, Robbie," she murmured.

"Why is the answer always 'We'll see'?" Robbie complained, but he turned his attention to his dessert.

"Because October is a long time off, and lots of things might change by then," Kyle told him. He turned to Stephen. "Since you mentioned the lady in the kitchen, I think I'll pay my compliments to Mrs Andrews in person. She's outdone herself tonight. Is there anything you'd like me to tell her?"

Layne swallowed hard.

"It isn't Mrs Andrews," Robbie volunteered, cleaning his plate. "Mom fired her because she was mean and nasty."

Kyle's gaze rested thoughtfully on Layne. "Then who do we compliment for the excellent food? Layne? I didn't know you had so many domestic talents, my dear."

"Sorry to disappoint you, Kyle, but the credit isn't mine," she said quietly as she pushed her chair back.

"Then I really must meet the person in the kitchen." He left the room with Robbie trailing behind.

"I wouldn't worry," Stephen told her. "He's far more interested in the leftovers than the cook's credentials. As a matter of fact, the leftovers *are* the cook's credentials."

Layne laughed. "Shall we have coffee, or wait for them?"

"Oh, let's have coffee, by all means. It may be hours before they've finished sampling." He propelled his wheelchair towards the library.

As they entered, Jessica Tate looked up from the magazine she was flipping through. She had carefully arranged herself in a casual pose in one of the deep upholstered chairs in front of the fireplace.

She was wearing a snappy cocktail dress in teal blue with a single shoulder strap. Few women could have carried it off, but on Jessica it looked dashing. Her hard blue eyes took only an instant to inspect Layne from head to toe. "Oh, dear," she sighed. "I suppose I should warn Cam."

Layne ignored the thrust. It's jealousy, she told herself; Jessica had assumed she would be Kyle's hostess, and she was getting even. At least there was something about her that Jessica was jealous of; it made Layne feel better. She crossed the room to where the coffee tray stood.

Jessica followed her. "Why did you even come back, Layne?" she asked in a low, tight voice. "Don't you understand that you aren't wanted at Wheatlands?"

Layne ignored her. She poured Stephen's coffee and carried it to him.

He looked unhappy, though she didn't think he could have heard Jessica's last remark. When she offered him the coffee, he shook his head. "I'm sorry, dear," he said, "but I'm more tired than I thought. If you'll excuse me?" His eyes shifted from her to Jessica and back.

Layne walked down the hall to the elevator with him. "I feel like a deserter to leave you alone with her," he said, "but I can't bear to listen to her. Now that Kyle has his family back, she should have the decency to stay away. Why can't the girl take a hint?"

Probably because Kyle isn't dropping any, Layne thought. But she just kissed Stephen and wished him good night and waited till the elevator purred towards the upper floor before she went back to the library.

The door was half-open, and she could hear a heated discussion. Kyle and Robbie were still arguing over a close call in the last baseball game they'd seen. Layne thought the discussion had passed the point of reason on the first day, but as she stood in the doorway she heard Jessica's trilling laugh. "He's so cute, Kyle," she gushed.

Layne pushed the door open. "Robbie, it's bedtime," she said.

Robbie made no protest. In fact, he said nothing at all until he was tucked in. Then he frowned. "Why does Jessica act like that?" he wanted to know. "And why does Dad like to have her around?"

"I don't know," Layne answered steadily. "Why don't you ask him?"

He sat up in bed. "She's like Gary!" he said triumphantly. "Are you going to see Gary any more?"

I've never lied to him, Layne reminded herself. "No. Not as long as I'm at Wheatlands."

He frowned and thought it over. "Are you and Dad going to get divorced?" he asked finally.

"Why do you ask that, Robbie?"

"Sometimes after you tuck me in at night, I get up again," he admitted. "I sit in that little corner at the top of the stairs, and sometimes I can hear you when you're in the library. You argue a lot."

"Every couple argues sometimes, Robbie."

He frowned again at that, but Layne didn't give him a chance to notice that she hadn't answered his question. She pulled the sheet up around him, stopped beside the big velvet dog bed to scratch Beast's ears, and turned out the lights.

There was no point in going downstairs again, she thought. She was no martyr, and she didn't care to intrude on Kyle and Jessica. So she went to the sitting room and found a book to pass the rest of the evening.

The maid tapped on the door. "Mrs Emerson? There's a telephone call for you."

Layne looked around, and realised that the closest phone was the one in Kyle's bedroom. She put her book down and went to answer it.

"Layne? It takes them long enough to find you. What do you do around there, hide?"

"Hi, Gary." Her tone was cool, and she sat down on the very edge of the big bed.

"I'm lonely for you, Layne. I know you don't like for me to call you, but I just had to talk to you tonight."

"This isn't very good timing, Gary, Kyle may walk in at any moment."

"His convenience certainly comes first with you doesn't it?"

"It isn't a matter of his convenience," Layne tried to explain. She walked across the room, trailing the long phone cord, to look out the window. Jessica's car was still parked in the drive, she noticed. "Gary, I'm just trying to avoid trouble for myself. He'd be upset if he knew you were calling me, and I can't blame him.''

''Don't you think it's about time you got honest with Robbie and told him what's going on? If you'd just quit playing games, we could at least get our feelings out in the open.''

''I've told you before, Gary, that I'm not comfortable with the idea of being married to one man and engaged to another at the same time. So our feelings—whatever they are—will have to wait.''

There was a brief silence. ''You don't understand how difficult it is for me, do you? I love you, and it isn't easy to sit here thinking about you living with him.''

''I know it isn't easy.'' Layne tried to keep her voice level. ''It's not exactly a picnic for me here either.''

''You certainly seem to be enjoying yourself. Having the governor pop in for tea…''

He sounded like a whiny child tonight. It was hard for him, Layne admitted; it was a difficult situation for everyone. If it had been Gary who had moved in with his ex-wife for a summer, Layne would have been just as upset.

Or would she? She stared out of the window, so absorbed in her thoughts that it took a minute to realise that Jessica's car was pulling away from the house. She'd better get off the phone quickly. ''Gary, please don't call me back. I'll get in touch with you when I can. I have a lot to think about.'' She hung up without giving him a chance to answer.

She was barely back in the sitting room when she heard Kyle moving around next door. She sighed, and smiled, and started to get ready for bed.

She had her bed made on the long couch before she realized that she had left her pillow in Kyle's room that morning. There was nothing to do but retrieve it. The couch was uncomfortable enough with a pillow; sleeping there without one would be impossible.

She tapped once on the bedroom door and walked in. She stayed out of his way as much as possible, but a certain amount of intimacy was inevitable. More than once she had walked in just as he'd got out of the shower. It didn't seem to bother Kyle, and Layne had learned to ignore his presence because when she became embarrassed it simply amused him.

Halfway across the bedroom it occurred to her that if she walked in, picked up her pillow, and left, she might as well stand there and scream that she had slept in his bed last night. So she detoured towards the dressing table and sat down to brush her hair.

Kyle was still fully dressed in dinner jacket and dark trousers. "Why didn't you come back downstairs?" he asked.

"I didn't feel that it was necessary. You're quite able to entertain Jessica without me."

"You could have been polite."

"Why? She isn't."

"It's the obligation of the hostess."

"I think that would have aggravated Jessica even more." Layne turned her attention to straightening out the mess on the dressing table.

He shook his head, but dropped the subject. "I checked on Rob," he announced. "He's sound asleep, and Beast is guarding him."

"They're both happy." A little awkwardly—why would he care what she thought?—she added, "I'm glad you changed your mind."

"Something told me the next time Beast ran away Robbie was going with him."

"That's possible," Layne conceded.

Kyle pulled off his tie and draped it across the top of his dresser. "Were you planning to tell me about firing Mrs Andrews, or did Robbie let something out of the bag at dinner?"

"I would have told you. How on earth could I have kept you from finding out? I just wanted to wait till Mrs Kirk had a chance to prove herself."

"She did that. The hot rolls almost melted in my mouth. And far too many of them, too," he added, ruefully patting his stomach. "Why did you fire Mrs Andrews?"

"Because she made some remarks about our living arrangements in front of Robbie."

He removed the pearl cufflinks from the formal shirt and started to unbutton it. "Sensitive subject, Layne?"

"It was upsetting Robbie; that's sensitive enough as far as I'm concerned." Layne started to rub moisturiser into her skin. "Besides, she was stealing from the household money."

"I don't suppose you can prove that."

Layne shrugged. "No, but I know it. And you would too if you paid any attention. However, if you'd like to hire her back..."

He waved a hand. "No, I don't think that's necessary. But this new cook of yours sounds too good to be true. You'd better watch her closely."

"I'll be delighted to. For the next five weeks; after that it's strictly up to you."

"I'm surprised you aren't counting it down to days yet. Living here is a real trial for you, isn't it, Layne?"

"It's worth it to be with Robbie."

He hesitated for a second as if he wanted to say something, then shook his head and took off his shirt. Layne tired not to look at him, but she couldn't help seeing the broad, tanned chest. It was covered with soft dark hair that had cushioned her head on so many nights. She sighed and pushed the thought away. That sort of memory would bring her nothing but trouble.

"What will you do after you leave here?"

"I don't know. Do you have any suggestions?" Her tone was as flippant as she could make it. As if he cares, she thought. Kyle doesn't care where I go or what I do, as long as I stay as far as possible from Robbie.

"I might. I'll think it over. We might find you a job at Emco; you're a good typist."

"Thanks," Layne said dryly. "But I can do without a job that someone has to manufacture for me. I'd rather get my own, and it won't be at Emco."

Kyle shrugged. "Suit yourself. Did you see Gary while I was gone?"

Layne was wary. "As a matter of fact, I did."

"Did you sleep with him?"

She controlled the nervous tremor in her hand and said with careful casualness, "Would you believe me if I said no?"

"Probably not. I just wanted to see what you would say."

Layne tipped the bud vase on the dressing table so she could sniff the single yellow rose. "If it will put your mind at rest, I will be married to Gary before I ever sleep with him."

Kyle was silent for a few minutes. "Does that mean that you're engaged to him?"

"How could I be? I'm still married to you."

"I wondered if you really remembered that fact. I'm relieved that you do."

"How could I forget it?" She put the cap back on the

bottle of moisturiser and reached for the night cream. She wished that she could just walk out of the room, but Kyle would think she was running away from him. And, she admitted, she probably would be.

"You still believe in the good old double standard, don't you, Layne?"

She turned around on the small stool at him. "What does that mean?"

"You won't sleep with Gary because you aren't married to him, even though you say you love him."

"You sound as if you're complaining."

"And you won't sleep with me—even though you are married to me—because you don't love me. Different excuses for different people. Each man has to play by a different set of rules."

"You made the rules, Kyle."

"Then let's change them. I miss having a woman in my bed, Layne."

"How unfortunate for you." She carefully patted night cream on to her nose. She had sunburned the sensitive skin a little, she saw. "I'm sorry to have to decline the invitation, but I have no desire to repeat the mistakes of the past."

"Were they mistakes? One of those romps resulted in Robbie, and you wouldn't change a hair on his head." He came across the room and stood behind her, studying her face in the mirror, his hands firm on her shoulders. "Besides, it was fun, Layne. Why shouldn't we have that kind of fun again? What's to stop us?"

"For one thing, the fact that I do not want to sleep with you." Layne shrugged his hands off her shoulders.

Kyle laughed. "That's what you tell yourself. I like that nightshirt."

She had forgotten that she was wearing Robbie's gift

and no robe. The shirt was far too large, but it was just the kind Layne liked to sleep in.

"You never used to wear anything at all to bed," he mused.

"It was different when we…"

"My darling Layne, we are still married. Remember? You just told me a few minutes ago." His hands brushed over the soft knit of the shirt, his touch featherlight over her breasts. Layne drew a quick, uneasy breath, but his hands slipped down to her waist, holding her firmly against him. "That kitten reminds me of you."

Obviously it wouldn't remind him of Jessica, Layne thought. Jessica was a sleek jungle cat—and Layne a very ordinary house kitten.

"Robbie knows the kind of thing I like."

"Meaning that I don't?"

"Quick, aren't you? I just meant that you haven't been around enough to notice what I like."

"You sound jealous, darling," he said. His voice was soft and teasing. "I'll take better care to stay home and pay attention. Very close attention."

"That wasn't what I meant…" Layne stammered.

Kyle laughed. "And you have a very poor memory, Layne, if you think I've forgotten the things you like." He picked up the dinner jacket he had discarded and hung it in the wardrobe. "I remember all kinds of things you like."

There was an undertone to his voice that made Layne shiver. He had always had the power to make her want him. It frightened her to know that he could still do it.

But he changed the subject, and she breathed a little easier. He had just been teasing, after all. "What are you going to wear for our dinner party for the governor?"

"Clare's dress."

She saw the frown that began to gather around his eyes, and quickly became intent on the single stray hair that needed to be plucked from her left eyebrow.

But his voice was gentle as he asked, "Why do you continue to call it Clare's dress? She gave it to you."

"All right," Layne said amicably. "I plan to wear my orange dress—the one Clare gave me."

The silence dragged out. Layne sneaked a look at Kyle. He was standing, hands on hips, regarding her thoughtfully. Seeing the muscles in his shoulders and arms made her uneasily aware of how strong he was.

Then he said, "And the garden party? What are you wearing for it?"

He wasn't gong to like this, she knew. "My blue sundress." She held her breath and plucked the offending eyebrow hair, pretending to be engrossed in the chore.

But there was only silence. When she finally dared to look at him, he was rummaging through her wardrobe. "This one?" he asked pleasantly, holding it up as if to assess it.

"That's the only blue sundress I own," Layne pointed out.

He took a better hold of the neckline as if to inspect it, and ripped the dress down across the front from neck to hem. Then he brought it across the room and flung it in her lap. "I'm terribly sorry, Layne," he said. "I'm afraid my hands slipped."

She stared, horrified, at the wreck of the garment. Even though she had grown to hate that dress over the last few weeks, it had been hers, and Kyle had wilfully destroyed it. "Kyle, you can't just rip up my clothes if they don't suit you!" she raged.

"Can't I? It seems to me I just did."

Tears flooded her big eyes. "You had no right to tear up my clothes."

"I have every right to insist that my wife dress appropriately. So when you go shopping, be certain that you buy something suitable for the garden party. And while you're at it, something new for the dinner would be a nice idea."

"Why does it matter so much?" she demanded. She slid around on the dressing table bench to face him. "In another five weeks I won't be here any more. What difference does it make what dress I wear to your precious garden party?"

"It matters because you're too pretty to hide yourself in muddy colours and badly styled clothes."

"That doesn't matter a damn to you, Kyle," she flashed. "It would hurt your pride if I wasn't dressed to your standards when the governor came. It might make him wonder what you ever saw in me."

"He certainly would wonder if he saw you in your ordinary clothes," Kyle retorted. "I think if I ever see another T-shirt on you I shall rip it off." His voice was hard.

"It hurts you to look at me, doesn't it, Kyle?"

He looked at her with a sudden dawning of comprehension. "Is that why you do it, Layne? Do you plan to make yourself look awful because you think it bothers me to see you that way?"

"No, I don't delude myself. I don't matter to you at all; you wouldn't care what I looked like if I wasn't still your wife. But you're too proud to admit that Mrs Kyle Emerson might not be a beauty. Well, I'm not ashamed of my looks, and I'm not going to pretend to be something I'm not."

"But you are pretending, Layne. You're hiding behind a wall of badly chosen clothes. You're afraid to be a woman.''

''I'm not the sort of woman Jessica is, that's sure.''

He smiled grimly. ''That is certainly true.''

She flinched as if he had struck her.

He came across the room slowly, and Layne felt herself shrink. ''Do you know what I think you need?'' he asked.

''I'm sure you're going to explain it to me.''

He smiled. ''First you need a good spanking, but since I'm not your father I'll have to pass on that. Then you need to be reminded of how it feels to be desirable.''

''And I suppose you think that's your function in life?''

''I am your husband.''

''That's a mere formality.''

He took the tweezers out of her hand and replaced them on the dressing table. ''It doesn't have to be a formality, Layne. We're both adults, and it's a long time till Labor Day. Why shouldn't we enjoy each other?''

''Why don't you just go and enjoy Jessica? I'm certain it would do you both good. She looked very frustrated tonight.''

He smiled and pulled her up till she stood in the circle of his arms. ''You can't deny that we had something unusual. Making love to you was as natural as breathing. You set me on fire, Layne. You still could, you know.''

Layne's voice was unsteady. ''Sorry, I've forgotten where I left my matches.'' She tried to pull away, but it was impossible; the strength he had developed with years of manual labour held her prisoner.

''Remember what it was like, Layne?'' he murmured. His lips brushed her cheek, her temple.

She shivered. ''Stop it, Kyle.''

"Why? Don't you like to remember? You were such an eager little bride that you would wake me at dawn so we could make love before I went to work. I see you do remember; you're blushing."

She turned her head sharply so he couldn't see her face. But Kyle merely changed his tactics slightly, bending his head to kiss the nape of her neck under the glossy brown hair. The path his mouth followed seemed to burn.

"Do you miss that, Layne? Are you happy sleeping on your lonely couch? Or would you rather be here with me?" The question was husky.

"Going to bed together was the only thing we had in common, Kyle. It wasn't much of a foundation for marriage then, and it certainly isn't anything I need now."

But her voice sounded desperate, and he knew it. "Are you certain you don't need me? How long has it been, Layne? It seems—too long. Far too long."

He picked her up; the small bench fell over with a crash as her foot caught in the rung.

The bed was already turned down; his touch was gentle as he put her in the centre of it. "Layne..." he groaned as he pulled her into his arms.

She tried to turn her head to avoid his kiss. "I'm surprised you even remember my name."

"Layne, I need you. I need to make love to you tonight."

"The key word is 'tonight,'" Layne agreed, "and I'm not having any."

In the sudden silence his hold loosened, and she pulled free and stalked across the room.

Once in the sitting room, she leaned against the doorframe, eyes closed in relief. It might be false security with only a door between them, but she had escaped from the trap he had tried to snare her in. She was safe again, at least for tonight.

The door opened behind her and she whirled around, eyes wide in shock.

Kyle laughed grimly at her fright. "I didn't come to drag you back into bed, Layne," he growled. "I like my companions to be willing."

"Then why are you here?"

"Because you forgot your pillow. That was what you came for, wasn't it?" He thrust it into her arms. "Here—enjoy your cold, lonely couch. And remember, when you can't sleep, that you are the one who chose to live this way."

She didn't sleep, of course. Kyle's angry face kept popping up in front of her, and she tossed on the narrow couch, trying to escape from him. When she finally tumbled into exhausted slumber, though, it was to dream of a Kyle who was not angry, but who was still every bit as frightening.

She had never denied his attractiveness, but why was he stalking her dreams, she wondered wearily. Then she came awake abruptly as her blanket was pulled away.

Kyle was standing over her, trim and well-groomed in grey slacks and a black silk shirt. "You've got five minutes to get dressed, Layne," he told her firmly. "We're going out."

She was too sleepy to argue, and his tone of voice told her that she would have little success if she tried. So she put on the first clothes that she could reach—a low necked knit shirt and cut-off jeans—and ran a comb through her hair.

His jaw tightened when he saw her costume, but he didn't comment.

"Can I at least have a cup of coffee?" Layne asked plaintively.

"Later." He hurried her out to the Cadillac.

"Where are we going?"

"Over to North Winds, where you are going to buy some clothes."

She opened her mouth to argue, but the look on Kyle's face quickly convinced her that it would be safer if she capitulated. "All right. You owe me one for tearing up my sundress." Her tone was combative.

He didn't bother to answer, didn't even speak again until they were inside the mall. At the door of the boutique, Layne stopped.

"What is the matter with you now?" Kyle asked impatiently. "If you're planning to throw a public tantrum, Layne, I warn you that I'll treat you the same way I would treat Robbie."

She waved a hand towards the racks of clothes. "If this is Jessica's shop, I am not going in," she said quietly. "And I don't care what you do to me."

"It isn't." He took her arm in a firm grip, and Layne let herself be pulled into the shop.

He had obviously talked to the saleswoman in advance, because she came up with a smile. "Good morning, Mrs Emerson," she gushed. "Something for a garden party, I believe? I think we have just the thing for you." She swept Layne into a fitting room where a half-dozen dresses were waiting.

She tried them all, liked two, and stood biting her lip as she tried to decide between them. In the old days, she'd have compared the prices, but there were no tags on these dresses. It was the kind of place, Layne thought, where if you had to ask how much it cost, you couldn't afford it. Unless, of course, Kyle had asked that the tags be removed, so she couldn't use price as a guideline.

"Why don't we let Mr Emerson look at them?" the saleswoman asked helpfully, and before Layne could protest the two dresses were being displayed to Kyle.

He glanced from one to the other. "That one," he said, pointing to a severely plain pumpkin-coloured dress with a halter top. "It's more suited for a party."

Her eyes rested lovingly on the other dress, an oyster white shirtdress with chocolate-brown piping on the sleeves and matching buttons and belt. But she nodded at his choice; he was right.

"She'll take both of them," Kyle told the saleswoman.

"No, I won't. You owe me one dress, not two."

Kyle ignored the interruption. "And now a dress for a very formal dinner party."

Layne opened her mouth to protest. "You're wasting your money, Kyle," she warned him. But he was looking over her shoulder, and he didn't seem to hear.

Layne turned to see what had drawn his attention, and saw a mannequin wearing a lacy long dinner dress the exact shade of ripe apricots. Kyle looked from it to her with a long assessing gaze.

The saleswoman, who was no fool, was already checking the tags. "It's a one-of-a-kind item, Mrs Emerson," she announced. "And it's your size."

Layne shook her head, but somehow she found herself in the fitting room wearing the dress anyway.

It was far too revealing, she thought, despite the deceptively demure high neckline. Her shoulders were covered by a brief, lacy cape, but her back was bare except for a T-strap of lace that pretended to conceal her spine.

The skirt fell softly from a shirred waistline. The whisper-fine fabric breathed elegance against her skin.

And it did marvellous things for her figure. Layne felt like a fashion model in the dress.

"How much is it?"

"It's just three-fifty, Mrs Emerson. And it is the only dress like it. It's from our exclusive collection."

Three hundred and fifty dollars certainly sounded exclusive to Layne. "No dress is worth that kind of money."

"Let's show it to Mr Emerson," the woman urged, and Layne found herself face to face with Kyle.

"Like it?" he asked.

"It's too revealing, Kyle."

He looked her over from head to toe, and Layne felt a slow blush spread over her as the inspection continued. Then he shook his head. "I think it shows off a good figure. And I imagine you know that, too. So what is your real objection, Layne?"

"It's too expensive," she admitted.

Kyle started to look dangerous. "Wrap it up," he told the saleswoman. "And have it delivered, along with anything else you think she'll need."

"But you don't even know what it costs," Layne protested.

"I don't give a damn what it costs. It looks better on you than any single other thing I've ever seen you wear."

"I won't wear it." But her hand was unconsciously stroking the silky fabric.

"Yes, you will. You'll wear it for that party next week if I have to put it on you myself. Understand, Layne?" His tone allowed no argument.

She believed him. If her appearance didn't reflect on

him, he wouldn't care what she wore, she thought. But Kyle would go to any length so that his wife would look the part when she played hostess to the governor. She told herself that she didn't care what his reasons were, but she felt as if there was a hole in her heart.

him, he wouldn't care when she wore, she thought. But Kyle would go on pinching pennies the way he could hock the gown which she saw at her mother to the governor. She told herself that she didn't care what the reasons were, but she knew it there was a hole in her heart

CHAPTER ELEVEN

WHEATLANDS seemed to sparkle, Layne thought as she slowly descended the massive staircase. Every window pane, every crystal chandelier, every piece of furniture had been polished, till the shine almost hurt her eyes. The great house was ready for the honour it would receive tomorrow, when the governor came to town.

The house would be ready for the party, but Layne wasn't so certain about herself. Her whole body was tense. I can't get by with this, she told herself. I'm just not good at this sort of thing. It isn't fair of Kyle to expect me to do this, anyway. I'll only be here another few weeks. And if he isn't back in time for the party tomorrow, I'll kill him.

But her second thoughts were more charitable. It wasn't Kyle's fault that the shopping mall under construction out in western Kansas had gone sour two days ago. He had no choice about the rush trip out there to salvage it. It was one of those things that always conspired to happen just when they were least convenient.

But if he didn't get home, and left her to entertain the governor by herself...

Layne reached the foot of the stairs and consulted her mental list. She had visited the florist; he'd be delivering the flowers first thing in the morning. She had stopped to talk to the caterer and tried out the food, which was delicious. It ought to be at the price, Layne's puritan soul remarked.

She still had to check with Mrs Kirk about the progress of the dinner party menu. And she still had a couple of hours of work this evening on the telephone, trying to reach all of the people who hadn't yet responded to their invitations...

"If I make it through this," Layne muttered to herself, "I deserve a year's vacation."

Her stomach tightened as if in agreement, just as she caught a glimpse of herself in the long hall mirror. She stopped for a moment to take an inventory. "Yes," she told herself firmly. "A full year's vacation. Somewhere far away from Kyle."

Mrs Kirk was kneading the dough to make rolls for the dinner party. She looked up with a flushed face as Layne came in. "The tea is steeping," she said.

Layne poured herself a cup and sat down on a tall stool. "What kind of rolls are you making?"

"The butterflake ones. They're Mr Kyle's favourite."

"How can you tell? Between Kyle and Robbie, they've never let a single roll or muffin or doughnut come back to the kitchen."

"I do like to see healthy appetites." The cook flipped the dough over and set it back in the bowl to rise. "But I know these are his favourite because the last time I made them he came out to the kitchen after dinner and asked if there were any more." She gave Layne a quick, conspiratorial smile. "When will he be home?"

"I don't know. When he called last night he promised to leave there early tomorrow morning, no matter what was going on. It's a six-hour drive, so he will probably come in with just enough time to change his clothes and meet Governor Howard."

"And then go back out there?"

"I suppose so, if he hasn't been able to straighten it all out."

"He'll be exhausted." Mrs Kirk shook her head.

Layne sipped her tea thoughtfully. "Promise or no promise, I doubt that he'll come home at all. He said last night that he trusted my ability to carry off the party if I had to—so I suspect that tomorrow morning he'll call to say he can't possibly come home."

"That would probably be the smart thing to do. After all, his business is more important than any party. He just wears himself out," Mrs Kirk sighed. "He doesn't eat properly—"

"What do you mean, he doesn't eat? He eats all the time."

"Unless he's here, he doesn't bother. He looks so worried, Mrs Emerson."

"I'm sure he'll be touched by your concern," Layne said lightly.

"Which is a polite way to tell me to mind my business." Mrs Kirk was unruffled. "Well, my business is to feed him, and in case he is here for dinner tomorrow, he's going to have what he likes."

Layne shrugged. "Just don't count on him being here. I'm not." She set the cup down. "I'll be in my office trying to call people. Why don't they respond to invitations?"

She was halfway down her list and having little luck when Robbie came in, Beast trailing behind him. Layne put the phone down with a sharp little bang—it was the fifth number in a row which had not been answered—and said, "Isn't it almost your bedtime?"

"Not for another hour." He pulled his baseball cap

tight down over his head, tipping his head back so he could look at her through narrowed eyes.

"I see that we're playing major-league pitcher again," Layne remarked. "And if you plan to be in bed in another hour, I would suggest that you start your bath now. There are so many layers of dirt on you that you'll have to soak at least that long."

"I just had a bath this morning," Robbie protested.

"I know. That's why baths don't come with guarantees."

"And I can't soak with the cast on."

"Then you'll have to scrub each layer off, and it will take even longer."

The telephone at her elbow rang sharply. Layne tried to ignore it, but after four rings she gave in. Obviously everyone else was busy. "Wheatlands," she said, and hoped that it was one of her stray invitations coming home with an answer. Or perhaps it was Kyle to tell her for certain whether he'd make it for the party.

"Layne?" It was Jessica's sharp, peevish voice. "When were you demoted to answering the phone?" Exactly the correct place for her, Jessica's tone seemed to imply.

Layne refused to get upset. "Kyle is still in Garden City."

"I know. I just wanted to make it plain, dear, that if he doesn't get back tomorrow, I'll take care of entertaining Cam. You won't need to disturb yourself about him."

"Are you suggesting that I hide in my room to get out of your way?"

"No, of course not. You'll have to stick around for the garden party, I suppose. But for brunch—well, you know that three makes such an awkward table. You do understand, don't you, Layne?''

''Oh, I know exactly what you mean, Jessica.'' she banged the receiver down and went back to her list. Jessica had all of the instincts of a hyena, she fumed.

She glanced at her watch. Surely Kyle should be calling soon.

Robbie had sat up straight when the phone rang, obviously hoping that it was his father. Now he slumped back in the chair. ''Her again?'' he groaned and chomped noisily on his wad of bubble gum.

''Cut it out with the gum, Robbie,'' Layne told him.

''Why don't you get rid of her, Mom? Now that you and Dad are back together, you sure don't need Jessica. Or Gary, either, Dad hates him.''

''Robert.'' She pulled the phone book across the desk. She'd promised to call Gary, and two days had gone by. Now was as good a time as any to get it over with.

Robbie pulled himself out of his chair. ''I suppose you're calling him,'' he said with great dignity. ''I'm going to take my bath.''

''Thank you, Robbie. I'll be up to tuck you in as soon as I finish talking to Gary.''

He grinned suddenly. ''In that case, I don't care how long you talk, Mom. Come on, Beast.''

She sat with the telephone in her hand for a long time, thinking about Gary. She had thought about him a lot in the past two days, and she had concluded that she could never marry him. It had nothing to do with Robbie's opposition; Robbie would object to anyone she married, if she and Kyle split up...

She caught herself and smiled. As if there was any doubt about that, she told herself. How glad she would be when all this pretending was over and she could just be herself again, independent and without responsibilities. That was why she didn't want to jump into another marriage. It would have to be a very special man who could tempt Layne to walk down the aisle again, and Gary Spencer wasn't it.

Gary didn't answer his phone. "And that's another sign, Layne," she told herself. If she really cared about the man, she'd wonder if he was out with someone else. But it really didn't matter to her who Gary was spending his evenings with. Or his summer, for that matter. If he had gone back to his ex-wife for the summer, Layne would have merely shrugged her shoulders.

She was glad that she knew that now, she decided, and felt a flush of relief spread over her. She might have slid without thought into a marriage with Gary, a marriage that would have been a disaster from the outset. Now she knew better. And whatever else resulted from this awful summer, she owed Kyle thanks for that.

Robbie was in his pyjamas, his makeshift bath over, Layne thought she would never be so glad about anything as she would be the first time she could put that child in a tub of bubbles and leave him for about a week, till every iota of dirt was gone. But until the cast was off, they would just have to make do.

"Am I clean?" Robbie asked as she inspected his ear.

"Approximately. But you'll have to work on it again in the morning, because you're not going to meet the governor with a dirty neck."

"He won't care."

"Perhaps not, but I will." She ushered him into the bed and tucked the sheet up around his shoulders. And, as she did every night now, she made a quick mental calculation of the number of times left to her to perform that simple chore. Less than a month now till Labor Day.

The cast would be off, Robbie would be back in school, she would be gone. "Good night, darling," she murmured, and her voice caught.

Robbie hugged her. "You miss Dad, too, don't you? Will he be home tomorrow?"

"He's going to try. The job he's doing is important and it's all tangled up, so he may not be able to come home for a while."

"I miss him." Robbie's voice was low. "It doesn't feel right to be here when he's gone."

"You'll get used to that. Wheatlands is your home now, honey."

"Will you stay in your room now, Mom?"

She was startled. "Why, Robbie?"

He ducked his head. "I get lonely when you go back downstairs. It feels like you're so far away. I don't mind so much when Dad's here, but..."

Layne glanced at the clock. "I think an early night would do me good, too." Her voice was unsteady. She felt warm all over when he needed her.

He grinned sheepishly. "Thanks, Mom."

She ruffled his hair, patted the dog, and went across the hall to her own room. She leaned against the door and yawned. At least tonight she didn't have to sleep on that awful couch. The last two nights, with Kyle gone, had been the best sleep she had got all week. She'd need it, with the governor coming tomorrow.

She pulled open a wardrobe door and took out a robe. It was nothing fancy, she told herself, but then she wasn't the type for fancy things. Not like Jessica, at any rate, who probably had a wardrobe full of silky négligés. And who no doubt kept Kyle in mind with every one she bought.

Layne fingered the pumpkin-coloured dress that hung next to the robe. She had to admit to herself that she was anxious to wear it. In that dress, she would look every bit as good as Jessica Tate.

Then she studied herself in the mirror and reconsidered. "The dress will look good," she told herself finally. And she would at least be presentable in it, even if she couldn't claim Jessica's elegance.

Her hand brushed against the other dress he had bought, the oyster white one with chocolate brown trim. She had been mightily tempted to wear it this morning. Kyle was gone; he would never know. But she had held firm. It was a matter of pride, after all, and Layne had plenty. She would wear the sundress and the dinner dress because if she didn't Kyle would carry out his threat. But he could not force her to wear the other dress. He had wasted his money.

She noticed that her hand was unconsciously caressing the nubby linen, and she closed the wardrobe door firmly to remove temptation. She hadn't realized how starved she had been for pretty things until Kyle dangled them under her nose. She wanted to look nice. No, it wouldn't require Kyle's threat to make her wear that lacy dinner dress. She'd love every moment.

A rustle roused from a sound sleep, and Layne sat up straight. In the shadows across the room, Kyle was unbuttoning his shirt. She could scarcely see him in the darkness, but there was exhaustion in the set of his shoulders and in the slowness of his movements.

"I thought you were coming in the morning," she said. Her voice was unsteady with sleep.

He turned and saw her sitting there. "Well, if it isn't

little Layne in the middle of my bed, and I'm too tired to do anything about it.''

Layne bristled for a moment, and then told herself that there was no point in starting an argument. ''I'll go into the sitting room,'' she said softly. It was a half-hearted offer.

Kyle rubbed a hand across his eyes. ''Don't bother. I can sleep on the couch for a couple of hours.''

''What time is it?''

''Almost four in the morning. We finally got the mess straightened out last night, and I left right away.''

He looked so tired that she just wanted to tuck him in. ''You can't sleep on that couch. You're too tall, for one thing. And it's uncomfortable.

He sat down wearily and took off his shoes. ''It doesn't sound very inviting. But I think I could sleep on a cement slab right now.''

''Kyle, stop arguing and get into bed, all right?''

''Does that mean you're not leaving it?''

''That's exactly what it means. I'm too lazy to go make up that couch, and I'm certainly too tired to argue about it. So we'll both just have to put up with the company.'' Layne punched her pillow back into shape and turned her back on him.

''You always did build yourself a nest, didn't you?'' Kyle commented. The mattress shifted as he stretched out beside her. ''Just like a puppy who worries his blanket around until he's comfortable...'' His voice trailed off.

Layne released the breath she had been holding and smiled ruefully at herself. So much for the irresistible impact that sharing a bed with her had on Kyle. She rearranged her pillow again and settled herself comfortably.

He sighed a little and turned over, curling himself around her body till his chest was firm against her back, one arm draped over her to hold her tight against him. It was the way they had always gone to sleep, she thought; their bodies remembered, despite the years of separation. A wave of longing swept over her. Those nights had been so beautiful...

Kyle's breath stirred her hair, and his hand moved slowly up under her sleep shirt to cup her breast. She drew a short, sharp breath. Was he asleep, she wondered.

Then his voice came out of the darkness. "I can't do it, Layne," he said. "I can't stay here beside you and not make love to you. And I'm not leaving."

"Then I will." Her voice was soft and breathless.

"You don't want to leave." He raised up on an elbow, and his mouth found the sensitive hollow at the base of her throat, then moved up to nibble at the tiny lobe of her ear. He slid the sleep shirt over her head so smoothly that Layne scarcely realised what he was doing, and as he tossed it aside he whispered. "You let me do that, darling. You could have stopped me."

Could she have? Layne asked herself. She could have fought him, she knew, but there was a curious weakness spreading throughout her body, a laziness that had nothing to do with being tired. Was this where she wanted to be, in Kyle's arms—in Kyle's bed?

"If you want to leave, Layne..." His hands were still; though he was holding her, she knew she could pull away. But she didn't, and after a moment his hold tightened, and he said, with a hint of triumph, "Remember how good it was, Layne..."

It was better. Their joining together was like the reuniting of two jagged, broken halves to make a perfect whole. It was so beautiful that Layne cried a little, afterwards, her tears absorbed by the dark hair on his chest.

And then they slept, exhausted, cradled in each other's arms.

Layne woke slowly, a warm, delicious glow spreading over her. She reached for Kyle, but found only empty space beside her in the big asleep. He had been so very exhausted. But not, she remembered with a small, secret smile, too tired to make love to her as if there was nothing more important in the world.

As she sat up and stretched, she saw him, already dressed, sitting by the wide windows with a cup of coffee and his newspaper. Before she could say good morning, he looked up with a frown. His face was drained, she thought.

"I hope you're not planning to stay in bed all day," he said curtly. "The governor's plane is due to land in half an hour."

"Jessica is meeting him," Layne said mildly. She couldn't even be jealous of Jessica this morning. "And it takes a solid hour to drive in from the airport." She pushed back the blanket and reached for her robe. "Would you pour me some coffee?"

He lifted the pot. "Are you certain you have time? Have you forgotten that we're supposed to go to Jessica's apartment for brunch?"

"I hurry much better after I've had one cup of coffee." Layne tied the belt of her robe, wishing that it was a satin négligé; something like that might waken Kyle's interest and remove the frown from his face. But even the old flannel felt like satin against her bare skin today.

She had forgotten how sensual a creature she was— or was it just Kyle who could remind her? He had always been able, with the slightest touch, to make her entire body tingle. But last night...

She shivered with the memory of it, and her hand brushed against his as she reached for the cup.

Kyle jerked back from her touch as if she had burned him. He wrapped both hands around his own cup and stared down at the front page of the *Wall Street Journal*. ''I'm sorry about what happened last night, Layne,'' he said. His voice was low and firm. ''I was so exhausted that I must have been out of my mind. It will not happen again.''

She stared at him, and the glory of the night shattered like a soap bubble. Woodenly, she raised her cup and drank, not even noticing that the coffee was scalding her mouth.

How could something that had meant so much to her be so meaningless to him? Indeed, so repulsive to him, for less than a week ago he had tired to convince her to sleep with him. ''We're both adults, why shouldn't we have some fun?'' he had said then. Now, after she had capitulated, he wanted nothing more to do with her.

She wanted to drag him out of his chair and batter her fists against that handsome face. Instead, she shrugged her shoulders and said, her voice perfectly clear and steady. ''Every woman learns to put up with it, sooner or later. It's quite all right.''

His dark eyes were like daggers as he stared at her. Then he set his cup down so hard that coffee slopped over the front page, and he strode from the room.

Layne refilled her cup with shaking hands. Did he hate her so much that any contact was repulsive to him? Or was he ashamed of himself for making love to a woman who wasn't Jessica?

Jessica. So much for not being jealous this morning.

Layne looked up at the pumpkin-coloured sundress hanging on the closet door and wished that she had the nerve to just run away. Let Jessica have Kyle, and Robbie, and Wheatlands. There was no contest anyway, nothing to fight about. Kyle had made his choice; why should Layne hang around until he decided that she had been there long enough? She was too proud to let him do that.

Tonight, she decided, she would leave. She would not give Jessica the satisfaction of being hostess at the garden party or the dinner, not as long as Layne was—in name if not in fact—the mistress of Wheatlands. She would perform those roles to the best of her ability, and then she would go.

Cooly, she brushed her hair till it shone, took particular care with her make-up, and inspected every inch of her appearance from head to toe before she approved the pumpkin-coloured dress. No one would have any cause to suspect that her decision was made, she told herself.

It felt good to know what she was going to do, to have her life back in her own hands, she thought as she slowly descended the stairs. Why had she ever let Kyle tell her what to do, anyway? To protect Robbie, of course, but she should have known what the result would be. History had repeated itself.

There was no point in going back over it all. Far more important was the knowledge that she was again making her own decisions. She ignored the dull pain in the pit of her stomach and went downstairs.

Robbie and his grandfather were in the dining room, both consuming ham and eggs with gusto, deep in a discussion of possible World Series contenders. Layne poured herself another cup of coffee, looked at the array of food on the sideboard, concluded that nothing looked appealing, and sat down across the table from the two baseball fans.

Stephen looked up with a smile. "You're quite this morning. Aren't you all excited about the parties?"

"I was never excited about them," Layne reminded.

"Robbie, get your mother something to eat. She can't entertain the governor on an empty stomach." He pushed his plate aside. "Kyle was in a little while ago. He looked fierce. I told him he should take you away for a while after all this nonsense. You both need a rest, Layne, and some time to get reacquainted."

Layne's hand clenched on the edge of the table.

"What do you want, Mom? Blueberry muffin? Ham and eggs? Bacon?"

"A muffin would be fine, Robbie." There was no point in arguing with Stephen; she'd just break up the muffin and play with it if she didn't want to eat it."

Robbie handed her a plate. "Are we going on a vacation? Where? I want to go to Disneyland."

"Robbie, you shouldn't plan on going along," Stephen told him.

Robbie looked horrified. "Why not?"

"Because your mom and dad need some time alone together."

"Away from me?"

Stephen smiled. "Rob, I realise you're the only child—but have you ever considered that it may not always be that way?"

Obviously Robbie had not. Utter astonishment spread across his face.

Layne found herself smiling. Poor little Robbie, the centre of his own universe, had never expected to have to share his father's attention, even with his mother, much less another child...

Another child. Layne's smile froze as, for the first time, she considered the possible consequences of last night. She had been absolutely unprotected against pregnancy, and she had never felt less lucky in her life. It was now even more important that she leave; if she was pregnant, and Kyle found out… Well, she'd leave tonight. And if she was pregnant, she'd worry about that later.

Stephen continued, "I thought you two might like a cruise. Or perhaps just a long, leisurely car trip—up through Canada or something. Or a couple of weeks at a resort. My treat."

"Stephen," she said gently. "If Kyle and I need to go away, we'll have plenty of things to choose from." She pushed the pieces of muffin around on her plate. Then, driven by curiosity, she asked, "What did Kyle say about it?"

"Just about the same thing you did." Stephen looked puzzled, and a little unhappy. "I don't understand why that boy won't leave Robbie with me and take you off somewhere and remind you of why he married you in the first place."

Because all the reminder I need is sitting across from me at this table consuming muffins, Layne thought. Kyle needed a son, and he has Robbie. No wonder he had regrets this morning about making love to me last night. He probably realised this morning that he might have a tough time getting rid of me. All he could accomplish would be to entangle himself further, and that he doesn't want.

Well, I don't want it either, she reminded herself. The sooner I get away from Wheatlands, the better.

* * *

The day was a blur in her memory. Episodes stood out, but the long day itself would be forever foggy.

She remembered Governor Howard's booming greeting, in his enthusiastic-politician voice, and Jessica's eyelashes fluttering coyly up at him as she hung on his arm. But they fluttered impartially at Kyle, too, and Layne could have cheerfully plucked each separate eyelash out.

And she would never forget the trill in Jessica's laugh as she monopolised the conversation at brunch at her apartment. It didn't help, either, that Kyle knew his way around Jessica's apartment so well, or that he automatically took over the role of host. Obviously, Layne thought as she watched him select a bottle of wine from the rack, he had done this many times before.

And what difference does it make? she asked herself. It was certainly no new discovery for her. But it hurt to have it made so obvious.

Cam Howard tried to pay equal attention to both women, but Jessica interrupted every time he asked Layne a question. Kyle didn't seem to know his wife was even present. Layne ate her omelette, but it tasted like cardboard.

Finally, Jessica tossed her napkin down and put a confiding hand on the governor's arm. "Oh, Cam, you're such a darling," she said. "I hate to break up the party, Kyle, dear, but isn't it time to go back to Wheatlands? After all, it would be awful if our guests arrived before we did."

Kyle smiled and agreed, and Layne could have thrown something at him. For an intelligent man, Layne thought, he was certainly dense when it came to Jessica Tate. "Our guests' indeed! Couldn't he see what she was doing? Or could he see only that Jessica was being extremely friendly with Cam Howard? That would explain why he was ignoring Layne; he was preoccupied by the frustration he felt over Jessica.

You just have to get through today, Layne, she told herself. Tomorrow you'll be free. Tomorrow Jessica won't matter.

She held tight to the conviction all through the garden party. Hundreds of Cam Howard's constituents showed up to drink tea and discuss their special interests, and it required every ounce of Layne's self-control to stay away from the triangle at the opposite end of the patio. The governor sat on the patio wall; Jessica hovered over him; Kyle was off to the side, watching Jessica whenever his attention wasn't being claimed by someone else. And across the lawn, tending to her duties as hostess, Layne found herself looking up time after time to see them there. Stephen saw them too, and though he said nothing, Layne knew that he was watching her with concern in his eyes.

She slipped away from the dinner party to say good night to Robbie. She found him curled up on the windowseat, staring out over the festively lighted lawn where the caterer's men were still cleaning up the mess. He scarcely looked up as she came in, then turned his attention back to the limousines parked near the house.

Layne sat down beside him, careful of the delicate lace on her dinner dress. It was still a pretty dress, she thought, but it didn't hold the magic she had hoped it would. It was just a dress, and the party was just a party—to be survived, not enjoyed.

"I came to say good night, Rob. Would you like a quick story?"

He shook his head without looking up. "Not tonight."

He went over to his bunk and slid under the sheet without protest.

She followed to straighten the spread on his bed. It will be the last time I will tuck him in, she thought, and a cold shiver darted through her. How can I give up this child, she asked herself. "Sleep, well, darling."

Robbie didn't answer. Layne put a hand on his shoulder, and was stunned at the tightness of his muscles. She gently kneaded the back of his neck, and asked, "What's up, Rob? What's bothering you?"

It seemed for a minute as if he hadn't heard. Then he said, without expression and without looking at her, "Are you and Dad going to get a divorce?"

"What makes you ask that, honey?"

He looked at her then, blue eyes bright with tears. "You are, aren't you? That's what you always say when you don't want to answer a question." He dashed a hand across his eyes. "Dad told me today that you wanted to leave Wheatlands because you didn't love him any more."

Layne was furious. How typical of Kyle to put the blame on her for their breakup. But this time he had lied to that child who had never been lied to before...

He had lied when he said she didn't love him any more. The realisation was like a knife in her throat.

She did love him. God help me, she thought, I've always loved him.

CHAPTER TWELVE

AND what on earth was she to do about it? It was all very well to have suddenly concluded that she was still in love with her husband, Layne thought. But what could she do about it? She supposed she could walk back into the crowded room, throw her arms around Kyle, and announce to the group that she had seen the light... She could imagine the look of disgust that would appear on Kyle's face.

"Robbie," she said carefully, "sometimes even if two people love each other, it isn't enough." Why upset him by telling him more? He would know the whole truth soon.

"But what about me?" he cried. "What will happen to me?"

He sounded as if his heart was breaking, and Layne put her arms around him, trying to hold away the hurt. "You'll stay here at Wheatlands with your father. And I'll be around whenever you want to see me. You aren't losing me."

He gulped a breath, and sobbed, "But I love you both. I don't want to choose."

"Honey, I had you all to myself for eight years. Your dad missed that. It's only fair for him to have you now." There was no point in upsetting the child by telling him that his father would, if necessary, kidnap him.

"I have to stay here?"

She pushed the dark hair back off his hot face. "I thought you liked Wheatlands."

"I do, but not without you, Mom!" He was really sobbing now.

Layne's throat was so dry she thought it would be a miracle if she could make a sound. "Robbie," she managed finally, "we didn't have very much before we came to Wheatlands. I didn't have a job, and The Tank was wearing out, and..."

"I don't care about any of that! I..." He rubbed his eyes, and burst out, "I'll even go to day care!"

She had to smile at that, but her voice was deadly serious as she added, "You're right, honey. None of that is really important. But if I take you with me, you wouldn't see your dad, Rob. We'd have to hide from him, because he doesn't want to let you go."

He was silent then. She rubbed his back for a few minutes. "I'll come up and check on you later, Robbie. And always remember that I love you."

He looked up at her with tear-reddened eyes. "Will you be here in the morning?"

I have never lied to him, she reminded herself. "I don't know, Rob."

Cam Howard was doing his Harry Truman impression, playing pop tunes on the baby grand piano in the drawing room. He was good enough to make a living at it if he lost the next election, Layne thought absently, and realised that there, in a nutshell, was the reason she didn't think Jessica Tate would ever marry him. Jessica would take no chances on a husband's occupation, and politics was just too uncertain a field for her. She was, however, beside him on the piano bench, sitting so close that a sheet of paper wouldn't have fitted between them, a glass of champagne in her hand.

Layne asked the bartender for ginger ale, and stood sipping it thoughtfully as she observed her guests. Most of them were gathered around the piano, but even those who weren't didn't seem to need her attention. Kyle was across the room with a small, white-haired old lady, and as Layne watched, he threw back his head and laughed, and then came straight towards her.

She stayed where she was. If he wanted to talk to her, she reasoned, Wheatlands wasn't big enough to run away from him. And if he didn't, he'd just move her out of his way and do as he liked.

She watched his progress across the room, studying the set of his shoulders in the well-cut dark blue dinner jacket, the sun-weathered complexion, the dark hair with its tendency to curl. She clenched her hand around the cold glass; it would have felt so natural to reach out to him in one of those intimate wifely actions—to remove a speck from his lapel, to feel the strength of his arm under her hand, to brush her fingers down across his cheek.

Yes, she told herself, that sudden revelation upstairs had been correct. It wasn't just a physical reaction that she had been feeling all these weeks, though heaven knew that was part of it. There was a magnetism about Kyle that drew her, but it was even more than that. All this time she had been telling herself that it was only physical, that once she was away from him it would go away. But it would never go away. She loved him. All of him, even that sarcastic, cynical side of him.

Her thoughts were interrupted as he came up to the bar. He handed the bartender his glass and folded his arms on the edge of the walnut top. "You were upstairs a long time," he commented. "Is Robbie all right?"

"I didn't think you'd notice that I was gone."

"When the hostess disappears for a half hour, every-one notices," he countered.

That puts me in my place, Layne thought. She sipped her ginger ale.

"You aren't going to tell me, are you? That must mean that something is wrong upstairs. Perhaps I should go and check."

"Perhaps you should," Layne agreed quietly. "If you'll excuse me?"

She moved through the crowd, watchful of the com-fort of each guest, stopping to talk to one here and there. The white-haired old lady who had been amusing Kyle beckoned her over, and indicated a chair. Layne sank gratefully into it. "I hope you're enjoying yourself, Mrs Allen."

"Of course. It brings back the old days, when Kyle's mother was alive. She made Wheatlands the social cen-tre of Kansas City. Tell me, Layne—are you going to become a patron of the arts? We need some fresh ideas; it's been left to the old ladies too long."

A patron of the arts! It was the kind of invitation that the younger Layne would have jumped at, a chance to belong. Now—even if she wasn't leaving Wheatlands, it hardly seemed to matter. "I don't think so, Mrs Allen."

"A pity. Too busy with your family, I suppose. Well, it's obvious that you're doing a good job. I talked to Stephen this afternoon, you see. He thinks you're the single best thing that ever happened to the Emersons. You're all he can talk about—you and that little boy of yours. And I haven't heard Kyle laugh like that in years." She patted Layne's hand. "Whatever you're do-ing, dear, keep it up. But I do wish you could find a little time for the arts. At least join the Friends organi sations—that sort of thing."

"I'll think about it, Mrs Allen." Layne smiled and moved away. So Kyle was laughing a lot, was he? Well, Mrs Allen was hardly an impartial observer. And if he was happy, it must be because the parties were almost over and the summer itself was drawing to a close. This charade must have been a drain on him, too.

She really should wait to leave until she could say goodbye to Stephen, she thought. She didn't want to just run off, again, without a word to him. It would delay her departure just a few more hours. She would leave in the morning after Kyle had gone to work; it would be much easier than to risk a scene tonight.

"You must be worn out, Layne."

She turned quickly as Cameron Howard came up behind her. His shadow was nowhere to be seen; that probably meant, Layne thought, that she was hanging on Kyle's arm by now.

"Beautiful party; I can't thank you enough. You and Kyle will have to come to Topeka next autumn to celebrate when we get this legislation passed. I'll put you up at the Mansion and return the hospitality." He made his way through the drawing room one more time, with apologies for cutting the evening short.

The party dispersed quickly once Cam Howard was gone. Layne was grateful. Much more of that meaningless social chit-chat and she would just start screaming, she thought. Jessica, of course, was the last guest remaining. She and Kyle were standing by the long front windows, apparently absorbed in each other, when Layne left the room. There was no sense in causing a scene, she thought; there were still hired waiters and bartenders around. But she wondered, as she climbed the stairs, just how long it would be before Jessica and Kyle even noticed that she was gone.

Robbie was asleep, one arm flung up over his head, the cast hanging out over the edge of the bed. She gently rearranged him, covered him up, brushed her lips across his cheek. He sighed and murmured something, and frowned in his sleep. Surely, she thought as she crossed the hall, surely there was a better way.

The couch in the sitting room felt even harder and more uncomfortable after a few nights in the big bed, and Layne finally got up and sat in the window seat, curled into a ball, watching the moonlight that drenched the front lawn. She sat there and numbered her options.

The first option was stark and simple. She could take Robbie and run away from Wheatlands before Kyle's Labor Day deadline.

She sat there in the moonlight, her chin in her hands. She had no job, no cash, no car, no home to go to, no way to support herself and Robbie. She would be cutting herself off from the funds Kyle had promised her to get a new start. She would be separating her son from the father he had grown to love. And—''Let's be honest, Layne,'' she told herself—she would be separating herself from any contact with Kyle, and that would hurt.

She had run once before, with no more than the clothes she wore, and Kyle had not come after her, But he would search for Robbie. The only place she could go was to Clare, and Kyle would have no trouble finding her there. And when he found her—she shuddered as she thought about what Kyle would do to her.

So the first option was no choice at all. She turned to the second one.

She could leave Robbie behind when she left Wheatlands, either immediately, as she had planned out yesterday, or when Labor Day came and Kyle told her to go.

If she stayed and finished out her bargain, she'd be able to see him. Kyle had promised that if she cooperated, part of the price would be that Robbie could see her anytime he wanted. She would have some money, though that was the least of her concerns—she had started with nothing before, and she could do it again. And sometimes—surely sometimes she could see Kyle, too? After all, they both cared about Robbie. For his sake, there were things they would have to talk about, over the years.

If Robbie stayed at Wheatlands, he would have everything he needed, and probably a great deal that he didn't. He would have an education at whatever college he wanted; the fund that Stephen had already set up would make him a doctor or a lawyer or an architect—or all three, if Robbie chose.

But Robbie didn't want to stay at Wheatlands without her. He loved his father, but Layne was the only security he had ever known. He would not let go of her easily.

She'd stay till Labor Day, she decided. She would help him as much as she could over the next three weeks; by then, maybe Robbie would adjust.

She nibbled on a fingernail. Well, Robbie would simply have to adjust, she thought, for there was no other option.

Unless she stayed at Wheatlands.

"That's ridiculous, Layne," she muttered, and stared out over the lawn. But slowly the ideas was taking shape in her mind. Perhaps it wasn't so very ridiculous after all.

It would let Robbie have both of his parents. It would let Kyle have a happy Robbie, rather than a rebellious one. And it would let Layne have… "It will let me keep my son," she told herself firmly. She shoved aside the other reasons that lurked in the back of her mind. The only thing that mattered now was Robbie, she told herself, and squashed the knowledge that it was a lie.

And before she could lose her nerve, she went in search of Kyle.

The big bedroom was empty, and the bed had not been disturbed. She peeked into Robbie's room to see if Kyle might be there, and Beast raised his head with a warning "Woof!" Robbie whimpered a little as if he was having a bad dream, then subsided again into an exhausted sleep.

The house was quiet, and for a while Layne thought that Kyle must have gone out. Home with Jessica, perhaps. It didn't surprise her; if last night had ben a revelation to her, it must have also been to him. Perhaps he had come to realise that Jessica was more important to him than anything else could be. If that was so, Layne thought, perhaps he would be willing to bargain. If she could just stay with Robbie, she thought, she didn't care what Kyle did.

Then she saw the light coming from his study. The door opened at a touch, and she saw him sitting at the desk.

"Can't you sleep, either, Layne? It must be contagious."

She perched on the edge of a chair. "I've been thinking, Kyle, and..."

"God help us." With a steady hand, he refilled his brandy snifter from the cut-glass decanter at his elbow. "Would you like to join me?"

Layne shook her head. "How much have you been drinking?" she asked quietly.

"I've only started. But I doubt you came down here

to ask that." He looked at her intently over the rim of his glass, his eyes almost black. "You told Robbie that you wouldn't be here in the morning."

"I said I didn't know. But I changed my mind." She took a deep breath. "I came down to tell you that I want to stay at Wheatlands. I don't want to leave when Labor Day comes."

He set the glass down with careful precision. "Why?" he asked baldly.

"Because Robbie needs me. He won't be happy here without me. He loves you, but you're gone so much, and he needs stability in his life. He needs help to adjust to a new school and new friends. He depends on me, Kyle. I can't just walk out on him."

He was silent for a moment. "So you want to live here."

"Just the way it's been, Kyle. I know that giving up Jessica was difficult for you. I want you to know that I won't ask any questions about how you choose to live, if...if..." It all sounded so incredibly naive, even to her own ears.

"How kind of you. My wife is giving me permission to keep a mistress."

She kept her voice level with an effort. "I presumed that if you had wanted to marry Jessica you'd have done so years ago. If I'm wrong, and you are going to marry her, then I want to take Robbie away. He hates her, and he'll make her life miserable if you try to keep them under the same roof."

"I can't imagine you really care whether Jessica is comfortable."

"You're right, of course. I want Robbie to be happy." She finished lamely, "I want Robbie to have everything."

The silence was like a curtain in the room. Then Kyle sighed and said, "No, Layne." He pushed his chair back from the desk and stared out the window. "You may not stay here, and you may not take Robbie away. He would be no happier with Gary then he would with Jessica."

"I'm not going to marry him. Robbie and I will live on our own again."

He turned back to stare at her. "You'll give up Gary for Robbie's sake." It was not a question.

"Yes. I will do anything for Robbie. Please, Kyle!" She was pleading with everything that was in her, her hands clenched on the edge of his desk.

"That's where we're different, Layne. I love him too, and there are very few things I wouldn't do for Robbie, but staying married to you is one of them."

She cringed under the lash of his words. Finally, her voice so small that it was barely audible, she asked, "Then why did you bring me back here? Why didn't you just take Robbie a month ago and leave me alone?"

"Because I needed the answer to a question, Layne." He pushed the swivel chair back from the desk and turned his back on her. "I'd like you to go right now. Which hotel do you prefer? I'll reserve a room for you— my expense, of course, or won't you take that from me either?" There was a trace of bitterness in his voice. "Or are you going to Gary after all, since Robbie's not going with you?"

"Stop playing games with me, Kyle!" She was almost screaming. "What question? And what answer?"

He turned the chair back, just far enough to reach the telephone. "I'll call the Westin. I prefer the service there," he said thoughtfully. "I'm amazed that you don't already know the question, Layne. It was—why did you leave me? And the answer—'' He broke off and reached for the telephone directory.

"Why did I—but you know why I left!"

"I know that you were seventeen years old—hardly out of high school—and that you found yourself married and orphaned and pregnant in less than three months. You didn't know what had hit you."

"It wasn't the easiest time of my life," she admitted.

"And I wasn't much of a husband, was I? I was too busy building a future for us to worry about what was going on then. You had romantic notions of what marriage was all about, and when I couldn't live up to them, you left. I understand all that, Layne, but it doesn't take away the hurt." His voice was gruff. He really had been hurt, she realised.

She asked quietly. "If you wanted to know why I left, why didn't you ask me?"

He didn't answer. "You must have been very unhappy when you realised that Robbie was a miniature of me. It must have been salt in the wound every time you looked at him."

"It was," Layne agreed woodenly.

He didn't look at her, but his whole body seemed to tense.

"I wouldn't do it again, Kyle. If I could choose again, I'd stay." She knew with sudden clarity that it was the truth. Given the choice again that Jessica had thrown at her that day so long ago, Layne would not run. She would rather have Kyle, no matter what his reasons were, than not to have him.

"Because of Robbie." It was not a question.

"It does all seem to come back to Robbie, doesn't it?" she said, and suddenly she was blazingly angry. "If it wasn't for Robbie, I wouldn't be here. We wouldn't be having this argument. And you would be trying to figure out a way to break that damn will!''

"You're screaming again." Then he stopped short and put the telephone down with a bang. "What will are we talking about?''

"My father's, of course." She shifted in her chair. "Oh, don't pretend that you don't understand, Kyle. You were the executor, you certainly know what is in the will. If you aren't able to produce Robbie in court next year, you have to turn over Daddy's estate to charity, because the ten years is up. Remember?''

He was suddenly very still. "I'd forgotten.''

"Please, Kyle, I'm not dumb. Nobody forgets things like that. I know that you married me so you could have Daddy's business. And I know that if I'd stayed till Robbie was born you'd have kept him and kicked me out then. It's no different now—just nine years later, that's all.''

He wheeled the chair around again and pulled open the bottom drawer of an oak filing cabinet.

"If you're looking for the will, you used to keep a copy in the third drawer down, left side of your desk," Layne offered helpfully.

He ignored her, but a moment later he tossed a thick document across the desk into her lap. "I think you'd better read that. It was filed with the courts not long after you left.''

Layne glanced at the cover page, picking up words here and there. Robert Baxter Estate…Kyle Emerson, Executor…Petition of Bankruptcy… She looked up at him, horrified. "Bankruptcy!" she breathed.

"When Lucky died, Layne, he didn't have a nickel that wasn't borrowed from someone. The only thing he accomplished with that elaborate—stupid—will was to make me morally responsible for his debts. They were paid, by the way. Every last penny of them."

She was stunned. "I...I never suspected..."

"No one did. He had been sailing in dangerous water for a long time, and he'd always pulled himself through. That time, his luck ran out." There was a long silence. "So you read the will, and thought—what did you think?"

She covered her face with her hands.

His voice was relentless. "If you wanted to know about the will—" he mimicked her earlier question, "why didn't you ask me?"

When she remained silent, he sighed. "I loved you, Layne," he said finally. "I knew I was taking a chance when I married you. You were a child; there was no guarantee that what you thought was love wasn't just an infatuation. But I was certain that I could make you love me. I had a pretty high opinion of myself, didn't I?"

"If I'd stayed..." she breathed. She heard him walk across the room, but she couldn't raise her head to look at him.

He turned at the door. "But you left, Layne." His voice was heavy with exhaustion. "Take the car; it's yours. If you want to check into a hotel, charge it to me. Let me know where to send your clothes."

"You said I was just a child." Her voice was taut with strain. "Am I to be punished forever for a mistake I made when I was seventeen years old?"

There was a long pause, then the door clicked shut.

Layne started to cry, the frightened wails of a child who has just seen her world ending. She had played her last card, pleaded her least plea, and he had walked out.

Then his voice cut through her sobs. "Why do you want to stay here at Wheatlands?"

She held her breath, unsure for a moment that she had really heard him. She turned slowly, afraid that if she moved too suddenly he would disappear, like the illusion she was almost afraid he was.

"Because of Robbie?" His voice was harsh. His back was against the door, his arms folded across his chest. He looked forbidding, but there was something in his expression that compelled her to tell the truth.

"Because of you." Her voice was little more than a whisper. "If I have the choice, I won't leave again, because I still love you, Kyle."

He didn't move. Finally he said, "You cried last night when I made love to you."

"Was that why you were so cold this morning?" she asked carefully. It was hard to breathe.

"It does wonders for a man's ego when the woman in his bed bursts into tears." His words were heavy with sarcasm.

"Perhaps if it upsets him he should ask her why she cried," Layne said gently. "Sometimes I cry when I'm happy, when things are back as they should be..."

She didn't get a chance to say more. He pulled her out of her chair and into his arms, and for a few minutes Layne wasn't able to think, much less to talk.

"Do you mean it, Layne?" he asked finally.

"That I love you? That I have always loved you? I don't know how to prove it to you."

"I always wondered, you know, if you cared about me or if you just liked the idea of being in love. You were so young, and you hadn't many men to choose from. I didn't let you have a choice," he corrected himself.

Layne smiled. "That's a mild way to put it."

"I wanted you so badly," he explained, "and I was afraid to wait for you to grow up. Someone else might have come along." He was tracing her features with his fingertips, his touch featherlight against her skin.

"There is no one else, Kyle."

"I thought you left me because you needed to grow up and get that experience. And all those years, I hope that the next time I came home, you'd be here."

"I did need that time, Kyle. Those years on my own were good for me." Layne pushed a lock of hair back from his temple. The silver threads hadn't been there all those years ago. The years had taken their toll.

"I had stopped hoping. Then Robbie called me that day at the office." He held her a little way from him, his hands tight on her shoulders. "God, I was angry, Layne. You had no right to keep my son away from me, no matter whether you wanted to live with me or not."

"You're right," Layne murmured.

"So I decided to punish you, and I insisted that you come back to Wheatlands with him." He studied her for a moment and said thoughtfully, "The little girl I married would have been jelly in thirty seconds. But you had changed, Layne. Nothing upset you."

She felt tears pooling in her eyes, and put her head down on his shoulder.

"You didn't even react to Jessica when I kept throwing her in front of you. I finally had to admit that I didn't matter a damn to you any more, that the only thing that did matter was Robbie. No matter what I did, you just smiled and went serenely on, waiting for Labour Day so you could escape."

"I wasn't very serene inside, Kyle."

His arms tightened around her till she could hardly

breathe. Layne would have protested, except that it felt so good to be in his arms. "When I came home from Minneapolis that day, and you were waiting at the airport, I finally realised how much I wanted you to be waiting for me every time. I might have set out to punish you, but I had fallen in love all over again—with the woman you had become."

Layne remembered that passionate lover's kiss at the airport, and smiled. "I couldn't understand why you'd changed so suddenly. I thought it was just a new way to get even with me."

"Then when you continued to reject me, I knew I couldn't stand to have you here," he said. "Those years without you were hell, Layne, but it was worse to watch you every day and know that you preferred that awful couch to sharing my bed—that if it hadn't been for Robbie, you would never willingly have seen me again. And that so-called man you were dating..." He shook his head. "It really hurt to find that you preferred him to me."

"I wouldn't have married him. That was a habit, and as soon as I saw you again I knew I couldn't ever be happy with Gary."

He let her go and cupped her face in his hands, tipping it up so he could look into her eyes. "Can you be happy with me? Layne, are you doing this for Robbie?"

"Yes, I can be happy. And no, it's not because of Robbie." The words were simple and plain and direct, filled with every ounce of honesty she could summon. Whatever he saw in the depths of her eyes convinced him, and with a groan he pulled her back into his arms.

It was several minutes later before Layne regained the presence of mind to ask, "How did Jessica know everything that was in that will, Kyle? Did you tell her?"

"So it was Jessica."

"Of course it was." She let her fingers creep through his hair, delighting in the freedom to touch him again. "She still wants you for herself, you know."

"I never talked to Jessica about your father's business. But I did ask her husband's advice about bankruptcy. He was an excellent attorney, even if he didn't show very good judgment when he married Jessica."

"Oh." Layne relaxed. "She told me…"

"I can imagine what she turned it into. And I don't care. The next time I see Jessica I will tell her not to come to Wheatlands again unless she has an engraved invitation."

"That's not nice, Kyle. You did encourage her, you know."

"A lot of good it did me. You didn't care, and all I got out of it was several boring evenings with Jessica."

"You deserved every minute of it," Layne rubbed her cheek gently against his shoulder. "Robbie will be very happy. He wants us to stay together."

"Robbie can go to the devil. We're staying together because we want to, not because of that young imp. Right?"

Layne nodded. "No more lies…or playing games…"

"None. So where do we go from here?" He was fighting a yawn as he spoke.

"Up to bed."

"Marvellous idea."

"So you can get some sleep. And tomorrow we'll decide what to do next."

"Three years on a desert island sounds good. Do you think my father will babysit?"

"I think he'd be delighted."

They walked together up the big stairway, arms

around each other. Neither of them saw the little boy and the big dog, hidden in the shadow of the alcove at the top of the stairs. But the boy and the dog saw them.

"Looks like we finally got the job done," Robbie said. He put an arm around the dog's neck.

Beast just grinned and washed his master's face.

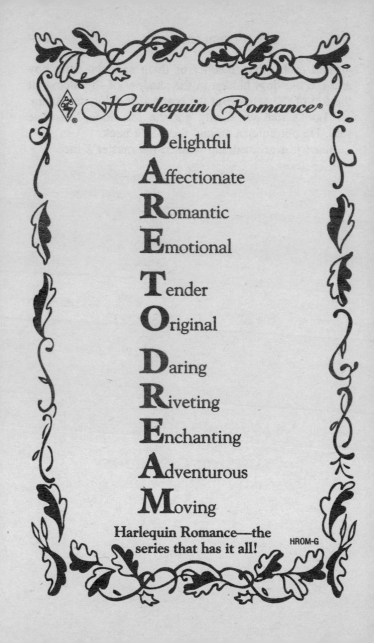

Harlequin Romance®

Delightful
Affectionate
Romantic
Emotional

Tender
Original

Daring
Riveting
Enchanting
Adventurous
Moving

Harlequin Romance—the
series that has it all!

HROM-G

HARLEQUIN  PRESENTS®

HARLEQUIN PRESENTS
men you won't be able to resist
falling in love with...

HARLEQUIN PRESENTS
women who have feelings
just like your own...

HARLEQUIN PRESENTS
powerful passion in
exotic international settings...

HARLEQUIN PRESENTS
intense, dramatic stories that will keep you
turning to the very last page...

HARLEQUIN PRESENTS
The world's bestselling romance series!

Harlequin® Historical

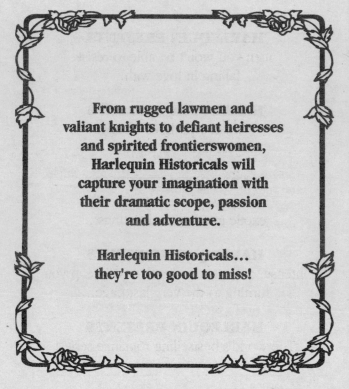

From rugged lawmen and
valiant knights to defiant heiresses
and spirited frontierswomen,
Harlequin Historicals will
capture your imagination with
their dramatic scope, passion
and adventure.

Harlequin Historicals…
they're too good to miss!

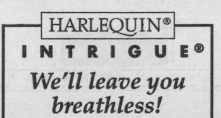

LOOK FOR OUR FOUR FABULOUS MEN!

Each month some of today's bestselling authors bring
four new fabulous men to Harlequin American Romance.
Whether they're rebel ranchers, millionaire power brokers
or sexy single dads, they're all gallant princes—and
they're all ready to sweep you into lighthearted fantasies
and contemporary fairy tales where anything is possible
and where all your dreams come true!

You don't even have to make a wish…
Harlequin American Romance will grant your every desire!

Look for Harlequin American Romance
wherever Harlequin books are sold!